Friendship
According to Humphrey

Betty G. Birney worked at Disneyland and the Disney Studios, has written many children's television shows and is the author of over thirty-five books, including the bestselling *The World According to Humphrey*, which won the Richard and Judy Children's Book Club Award, as well as a further twelve books in the *According to Humphrey* series, and nine books in the *Humphrey's Tiny Tales* series. Her work has won many awards, including an Emmy and three Humanitas Prizes. She lives in America with her husband.

Praise for Humphrey:

'Humphrey, a delightful, irresistible character, is big-hearted, observant and creative, and his experiences . . . range from comedic to touching.' *Booklist*

'This is simply good-good-good.' *Kirkus Reviews*

'An effective exploration of the joys and pains of making and keeping friends, which will strike a chord with many children.' *Telegraph*

'Children fall for Humphrey, and you can't beat him for feelgood life lessons.' *Sunday Times*

Have you read all of Humphrey's adventures?

The World According to Humphrey
Trouble According to Humphrey
Adventure According to Humphrey
(special publication for World Book Day 2008)
Surprises According to Humphrey
More Adventures According to Humphrey
Holidays According to Humphrey
School According to Humphrey
Mysteries According to Humphrey
Christmas According to Humphrey
Secrets According to Humphrey
Imagination According to Humphrey
Spring According to Humphrey

Three books in one!
Humphrey's Big-Big-Big Book of Stories
Humphrey's Great-Great-Great Book of Stories
Humphrey's Ho-Ho-Ho Book of Stories

Humphrey's Book of Fun-Fun-Fun
Humphrey's Ha-Ha-Ha Joke Book
Humphrey's World of Pets

Humphrey's Tiny Tales

My Pet Show Panic!
My Treasure Hunt Trouble!
My Summer Fair Surprise!
My Creepy-Crawly Camping Adventure!
My Great Big Birthday Bash!
My Playful Puppy Problem!
My Really Wheely Racing Day!
Bumper Book of Humphrey's Tiny Tales (4 books in 1)
Bumper Book of Humphrey's Tiny Tales 2 (4 books in 1)

By the same author

The Princess and the Peabodys

Friendship According to Humphrey

Betty G. Birney

FABER & FABER

First published in the USA in 2005 by
G. P. Putnam's Sons, a division of Penguin
Young Readers Group
345 Hudson Street, New York,
NY 10014, USA

First published in the UK in 2007
by Faber & Faber Limited
Bloomsbury House, 74–77 Great Russell Street
London, WC1B 3DA

This edition published in 2016

Typeset by M Rules
Printed and bound by
CPI Group (UK) Ltd, Croydon, CR0 4YY

A CIP record for this book
is available from the British Library

ISBN 978–0–571–32829–1

6 8 10 9 7 5

To Jane Birney de Leeuw, sister
and friend, and to Humphrey's
BEST–BEST–BEST friend and editor,
Susan Kochan

Contents

1 Strange Change

BUMP-BUMP-BUMP!

Mrs Brisbane and I were heading back to Longfellow School after the long winter holiday. But there were a lot more bumps in the road since the last time I rode in her small blue estate car.

'Now, Humphrey,' Mrs Brisbane said. She was interrupted by another BUMP! 'Don't be surprised.' BUMP! 'If there are a few changes.' BUMP! 'In Room 26.' BUMP!

My stomach felt slightly queasy as I hung on tightly to my ladder, so I had a hard time understanding what she was telling me. What did she mean by 'changes'?

'While you were at home with Bert.' BUMP! 'I came back to school to get things ready.'

I was at home with her husband Bert a lot over the holidays, and as much as I like him, I was worn out from running mazes a couple of times a day. Mr Brisbane loves to watch me run mazes. At least back in school, I could catch forty winks once in a while. And since I am a classroom hamster, I belong in the classroom.

My stomach calmed down a bit as Mrs Brisbane pulled her car into a parking space.

'Now, what about these changes?' I asked, but it came out as 'Squeak-squeak-squeak,' as usual.

'It's good to shake things up once in a while, Humphrey,' Mrs Brisbane assured me as she opened the car door. 'You'll see.'

I was already shaken up from the bumpy ride. Then a blast of icy wind made me shiver and I couldn't see a thing because Mrs Brisbane had thrown a woollen scarf over my cage. I didn't mind, as long as I was on the way back to my classroom, where I'd see all my friends again. Just thinking about them gave me a warm feeling. Or maybe it was the heat from the school boiler as we walked in the front door.

'Hi, Sue! Are we on for today?' a familiar voice called out. I couldn't see Miss Loomis, but I recognized her voice. Miss Loomis taught a class down the corridor. She was also Mrs Brisbane's friend.

'Sure, Angie. How about after morning break?'

'See you then,' said Miss Loomis.

Finally, Mrs Brisbane put my cage down in Room 26 and removed the scarf. When she did, I was in for a shock. Something unsqueakable had happened to my classroom! For one thing, the tables faced the wrong direction. They used to point towards the front of the room. Now they were sideways.

Instead of being arranged in neat rows like before, the tables were clumped together in groups. Mrs Brisbane's desk had moved to the corner of the room. Pictures of people I'd never seen before replaced the happy snowmen who had covered the notice board in December.

I was so dizzy from all the changes, I didn't notice the room filling up until Lower-Your-Voice-A.J. yelled, 'Hiya, Humphrey!' as he came out of the cloakroom.

Soon my other friends stopped by to say hello.

'Did you have a good holiday?' asked Miranda Golden. Miranda is an almost perfect human. That's why I think of her as Golden Miranda.

'My mother sends you her greetings,' Speak-Up-Sayeh said in her sweet, soft voice.

'Hey, Humphrey-Dumpty,' Garth shouted. That made Gail snigger, but I didn't mind. She laughed at everything.

At that moment, the bell rang. 'Class, look for your names and please take your seats now,' Mrs Brisbane said.

There was a lot of thumping and bumping as my classmates located their new seats. Now I had a better view of some of the students who used to sit on the opposite side of the room, like Don't-Complain-Mandy Payne, Sit-Still-Seth Stevenson and I-Heard-That-Kirk Chen. Maybe it is good to shake things up once in a while.

Then I noticed something odd. There was a stranger in Room 26, sitting near Sayeh, Gail and Kirk.

'Mrs Brisbane, she doesn't belong here!' I squeaked out loud. 'She's in the wrong room!'

Maybe Mrs Brisbane didn't hear me.

'Class, as you can see, we're making some changes this year. And one of our changes is our brand-new pupil,' the teacher announced. 'Come here, Tabitha.'

The new girl seemed SCARED-SCARED-SCARED as she got up and stood next to Mrs Brisbane. 'This is Tabitha Clark and I want you all to welcome her. Tabitha, why don't you tell us something about yourself?' The new girl looked down and shook her head. Mrs Brisbane quickly turned back to the class. 'We'll do that later. Now, who would like to be in charge of showing Tabitha around today?'

'Me!' a voice called out. Of course, it was Raise-Your-Hand-Heidi Hopper, who always forgets to raise her hand.

'Hands, please, Heidi. I think Mandy had her hand up first. Mandy, you will be Tabitha's buddy. I expect each of you to introduce yourself to Tabitha and include her in your activities.' She turned to the girl. 'I know you'll make a lot of good friends in Room 26. You may sit down now.'

The girl kept staring at the floor as she returned to her seat. She looked as if she needed a friend. I was so busy watching her, I only half listened to what Mrs Brisbane was saying. Was she really talking about 'poultry'?

'After all, this is Longfellow School,' she said. 'And as I hope you know, Henry Wadsworth Longfellow was a famous American poet.'

Poetry! Nothing to do with chickens or turkeys, thank goodness. I have to admit, I'm a little scared of things with feathers, ever since my early days at Pet-O-Rama. I still have nightmares about the day a large green parrot escaped and flung himself at my cage, screeching, 'Yum, yum! Time to eat! Bawk!' He was still shrieking as Carl, the shop assistant, carried him away.

That unpleasant memory was interrupted when someone blurted, 'I'm a poet and I don't know it. My feet show it – they're *long fellows*.'

'I-Heard-That-Kirk,' said Mrs Brisbane. 'Now, as I was saying, much of this term will be spent reading and writing poetry.'

The groans were loud. I guess some people are afraid of poetry, even without feathers.

Seth squirmed in his seat and pretended to pound his head on the table. 'Poetry,' he moaned.

'Sit-Still-Seth,' said Mrs Brisbane.

Sitting still wasn't easy for Seth. Now that he was practically right in front of me, I could see him wiggling and jiggling in his chair, which made Gail Morgenstern laugh.

'Stop-Giggling-Gail!' Mrs Brisbane warned.

Gail stopped giggling and started hiccuping.

'Please, go and get a drink of water,' Mrs Brisbane told her. She turned to the new girl. 'Tabitha, please put that toy away.'

Everybody stared at Tabitha, including me. She was cradling a scruffy teddy bear in her arms. The grey bear had cotton coming out of his ears and wore washed-out blue overalls with a button missing. Even his smile seemed a little faded.

'Now, please,' said Mrs Brisbane.

It was quiet in the room, thank goodness. I'm afraid that if Gail had been there, we would have heard peals of laughter and heaps of hiccups!

Tabitha slid the shabby bear under her table without a word.

Just about then, Mr Morales, the headmaster, marched through the door.

'Sorry for interrupting, Mrs Brisbane. I just

want to personally welcome you all back to school!'

The headmaster looked spiffy, with a tie that had little pencils all over it. He always wore a tie because he was the Most Important Person at Longfellow School.

'Thank you, Mr Morales,' said Mrs Brisbane. 'We have a new student, Tabitha Clark, and a whole new set-up for our class, as you can see.'

'Welcome, Tabitha,' said the headmaster. 'I'm sure you'll love it here in Room 26. I'm glad to see that our friend Humphrey is back as well.'

He walked all the way across the classroom to my cage.

'GLAD TO SEE YOU!' I squeaked in my loudest squeak.

'Hi, old pal,' he greeted me. He turned back to the rest of the class. 'You can all learn a lot from Humphrey. And I wish you a very successful term.'

After he left, I turned my attention back to Tabitha. She was still staring straight down. I couldn't see her face clearly, but it was almost as red as her copper-coloured hair. I guess I watched her for a long time, because suddenly the bell rang for break.

'Come on, Tabitha, let's get our coats,' Mandy said. Tabitha slipped the teddy bear into her pocket and followed Mandy to the cloakroom.

As soon as the students were gone, Miss Loomis

bustled into the room. Two pink dots of excitement coloured her cheeks and her curls bounced in all directions.

'Are you ready? Should we do it?' she asked Mrs Brisbane excitedly.

'Why not?' my teacher answered. 'I'll make room for him now.'

They walked over to the table in front of the window where my cage sits.

'Yes, he'll fit right here,' said Miss Loomis, pointing to a spot near my house.

Mrs Brisbane slid some of my supplies down to the end of the table. 'Now, you're sure he's not a lot of trouble?'

'Oh, no. Not nearly as much trouble as a hamster,' Miss Loomis answered.

WHAT-WHAT-WHAT? Not nearly as much trouble as a hamster! Since when have I caused any trouble in Room 26? Since when did I not totally dedicate myself to helping my classmates and teacher? Surprisingly, Mrs Brisbane didn't correct her. I was about to squeak up for myself when the bell rang again and Miss Loomis scurried out of the room.

I wondered who wasn't as much trouble as I am. 'He,' Miss Loomis had said.

He who? Curiosity made my whiskers twitch and my paws tingle.

My fur was practically standing on end as the

tables filled up. I saw Tabitha slip her bear out of her pocket. Heidi saw it too, and rolled her eyes at Gail, who almost giggled but managed to stop herself.

'Now, class, I told you there were some changes in our room this year,' Mrs Brisbane announced. 'Another of the changes is a brand-new classroom pet. I think he'll add a lot to Room 26.'

New classroom pet? Why did she want a new classroom pet when she already had a wonderful, terrific – OK, perfect – classroom pet, namely me? Was I being replaced?

Miss Loomis entered, carrying a large glass tank. I couldn't see what it was because my classmates were standing up, craning their necks, *ooh*-ing and *aah*-ing and chattering away.

'It's a frog!' shouted Heidi.

Miss Loomis put the glass box right next to my cage. Now I could see some water, rocks, and something green and REALLY-REALLY-REALLY lumpy.

'Meet our new frog,' said Mrs Brisbane. 'Miss Loomis will tell you about him.'

'Well, boys and girls, as you may know, we have a frog in our classroom. His name is George and he's a bullfrog. Before the holidays, one of our students brought in this frog to keep George company. We named him Og the Frog. Unfortunately, George didn't like Og. And being a bullfrog, George let us know he didn't like Og by making a lot of noise. That upset Og, I guess, because he would leap and splash all day long while George was croaking.'

My classmates laughed, but I didn't. On the one paw, I could see why George didn't want another frog to compete with. On the other paw, croaking at Og wasn't a very friendly way to act.

'With all the noise, we were having trouble getting any work done at all,' Miss Loomis continued. 'So I asked Mrs Brisbane if your class would like to have Og, and she said yes. He's a very quiet frog. Do you like him?'

My friends all yelled, 'YES!' Everyone except Tabitha, who was secretly petting her little bear.

Somebody went 'Ribbit-ribbit' in a funny croaking voice. It wasn't the frog.

'I-Heard-That-Kirk. That's quite enough. Og can provide the sound effects from now on. I think he'll make a nice friend for Humphrey,' Mrs Brisbane said.

A friend for me? At least he wasn't my replacement – whew! But I was already friends with every single person in Room 26, so she really didn't need to find me another one. Still, I didn't want to act unfriendly, the way George had.

After Miss Loomis left, Mrs Brisbane let the students have a closer look at Og.

Seth tapped at the glass.

'Don't do that, Seth,' the teacher warned him. 'You'll frighten him.'

'He doesn't seem frightened of anything,' Miranda observed.

'I think he's smiling,' added Kirk. 'That must mean he's *hoppy*.'

For once, Gail didn't giggle, which seemed to bother Kirk. 'Get it? Hoppy? Happy?' he tried to explain.

Gail rolled her eyes and groaned, which didn't make Kirk hoppy at all.

Mrs Brisbane called to the new girl. 'Come and see Og, Tabitha.'

Tabitha stared down at her table and shook her head.

'Come on, Tabitha!' Mandy sounded impatient.

Again, Tabitha shook her head.

'She hasn't wanted to do anything all day!' Mandy grumbled.

'Mandy –,' Mrs Brisbane warned her.

'Is he really a frog?' Richie stared hard at Og, who stared right back. 'Don't frogs live in water?'

'Some do,' said Mrs Brisbane. 'And some frogs live in trees. Og is a common green frog. He likes to live near the water, but not in it. That's why he has a tank that's half land and half water.'

A common green frog didn't sound very

interesting, but Og had certainly attracted the attention of my classmates.

'Can I take care of Og?' A.J. asked loudly.

'Lower-Your-Voice-A.J.,' said Mrs Brisbane. 'We will all take care of him.'

Once the students had returned to their seats, Mrs Brisbane held up a book on the care of frogs. 'We'll have to study this,' she explained. 'Taking care of Og will be quite different from caring for Humphrey. After all, Humphrey is a warm-blooded mammal. Og is a cold-blooded amphibian.'

Amphibian! That's nothing like a mammal. The very word made my warm blood run cold! I hoped that she would never ever put that word in a spelling test.

Mrs Brisbane looked through the book. 'Aha,' she said. 'It says that the common green frog is a medium-sized frog with a calm nature. It makes a distinctive twanging sound.'

'BOING!'

I almost fell off my ladder. What on earth could that noise be?

Then I heard another sound: the laughter of my classmates.

'That certainly is a distinctive twanging sound,' said Mrs Brisbane, looking puzzled.

'BOING!' This time the noise was clearly

coming from the frog. What kind of a way is that to talk? Aren't frogs supposed to say 'ribbit'?

Mrs Brisbane turned towards Og's glass box. 'Thank you for the demonstration, Og.'

Then I heard: 'Boing-boing-boing!' It didn't come from the frog this time.

'I-Heard-That-Kirk Chen,' said the teacher. She continued to talk on and on about amphibians and their life cycle.

'What does he eat?' Heidi called out.

'Hands, please, Heidi,' said Mrs Brisbane wearily. 'Mostly insects. Miss Loomis gave me a container of crickets.'

'Cool!' said Kirk.

Everybody else in the class groaned. 'Ewwwww!'

When I finished gagging, I squeaked, 'LIVE insects?' Not that anyone was listening to me. Especially not Og, who calmly sat there doing absolutely nothing.

At the end of the day, as the students gathered up their books and coats and filed past our table, at least half of them said, 'Bye, Og,' or 'Catch you later, Oggy.'

Not one of my classmates said goodbye to me. I suppose they all forgot.

Mandy stayed for a minute after class. 'Mrs

Brisbane, you told me to be friendly to that new girl, but she isn't very friendly back.'

'Don't-Complain-Mandy,' said the teacher. 'It's not easy to be the new kid in the classroom. Put yourself in her shoes. Give her some time. After all, we've got the whole term ahead of us.'

A whole term ahead of us – and I had to spend it with a frog?

Mrs Brisbane had shaken things up all right. And I felt queasy all over again.

> **The better part of one's life consists of his friendships.**
> Abraham Lincoln, sixteenth president of the United States

2 Upset Pet

I'd had bad days before. The worst day was when Ms Mac left. She was the supply teacher who found me at Pet-O-Rama and brought me to Room 26. She almost broke my heart by moving to Brazil, which is so far away.

I'd also overcome problems before. Like getting Mrs Brisbane and her husband Bert to go from not liking me to liking me a WHOLE-WHOLE-WHOLE lot.

But I'd never had a problem like this: how to make friends with a frog. Back in my early days at Pet-O-Rama, I'd met guinea pigs, mice, rats, gerbils and chinchillas in the Small Pet Department. If there were frogs around, they must have been over with the fish and other less interesting pets.

After school was over, Mrs Brisbane gathered up her coat, gloves and books, walked over to Og and me and said, 'Well, fellows, you're on your own tonight. Have fun!'

And with that she left.

I recalled the first night I was alone in Room 26. As it slowly got dark outside, I slowly got scared inside. I would have liked a friend to talk to that night. Maybe Og felt the same way. Like Tabitha, Og was new to the class, and I thought I should try and make friends with him. Mrs Brisbane had said it's not easy to be new. You should always listen to your teacher.

'Don't worry, Og,' I squeaked to him. 'They'll all be back tomorrow. And Aldo will be here later.'

I waited for an answer. All I heard was silence. I knew he probably couldn't understand me. Still, I'd learned to understand what humans said, and for the most part, they seemed to understand me when I chose to squeak up. Surely I could do as well with a frog. I decided to try again.

'CAN YOU HEAR ME?' I squeaked as loudly as possible.

Either he couldn't hear me or he was just plain rude. I couldn't see him all that well from my cage, what with my wheel, ladders, tree branches, sleeping house and mirror. Since I knew Aldo wouldn't come in to clean the room for hours, I decided to introduce myself. As an experienced (and well-loved) classroom pet, I could share my wealth of knowledge about the timetable, the students and the studies in Room 26. Og could come to me for advice whenever he wanted.

After all, you can learn a lot by taking care of another species, as Ms Mac told me. Surely that included frogs.

I easily opened the door to my cage. It has a lock-that-doesn't-lock. However, I'm the only one who knows about it. To humans, it looks like it's tightly latched, but trust me, it's not.

'I'm coming over, Og,' I announced.

Again, there was no response. I scampered over to meet my new roommate anyway.

The glass tank had a big dish of water on one side and pebbles and plants on the other. There was a screen on the top. Sitting under a large green plant was a large green lump.

I tiptoed over close to the glass and peered in.

The lump was even uglier than I first thought. At least compared with me. After all, I am a Golden Hamster with soft fur, dark, inquisitive eyes and a little pink nose. Intelligent humans such as Miranda Golden and Sayeh Nasiri have told me I am cute.

This Og thing, on the other hand, was a sickening shade of green with bulging eyes and not a bit of fur on him. Even worse, he had a huge mouth – as wide as his whole body – that curved up at the ends as if he were grinning. He didn't look happy, just creepy. I tried not to shudder.

'Allow me to introduce myself. I am your neighbour Humphrey,' I squeaked as politely as possible.

No answer. Maybe he couldn't hear me. After all, he didn't have cute rounded ears like me. He didn't seem to have ears at all. But at least he could see I was acting in a friendly manner.

'OG?' Stepping closer, I squeaked a bit louder this time. 'Even though we don't know each other, I'm happy to extend the paw of friendship –'

Then, with no warning at all, Og lunged right at me and let out a very loud 'Boing!'

I must have leaped a foot backwards! Og couldn't get through the glass, but goodness, he startled me!

'I was only trying to be friendly,' I told him, backing towards my cage.

'Boing!' He sounded like a broken guitar string.

I sneaked a peek at him. Was that grin a leer? Or a sneer?

My heart was still pounding as I darted back into my cage and slammed the door behind me. Some friend Og was, scaring me like that!

I tried to put myself in his shoes, like Mrs Brisbane said, but he didn't wear any. Neither did I, for that matter.

I grabbed the tiny notebook and pencil from

behind my mirror. Ms Mac gave them to me. No one in Room 26 knew about them. No one knew I could read and write. Writing helps me sort out my thoughts. And I had a lot of thoughts rolling around my brain that night – not all of them nice.

˙ö˙

I scribbled away for several hours and Og was pretty quiet, except for some annoying splashing. Goodness, I can manage to groom myself and get a drink of water without making that much noise!

Suddenly the room filled with blazing light and I heard a familiar CLANG-CLANG-CLANG. It was the Longfellow School caretaker, Aldo Amato.

'Be of good cheer 'cos Aldo's here!' a voice announced.

'Aldo! My friend!' I squeaked as I jumped on my wheel and began spinning happily.

Aldo parked his cleaning trolley near the door and clomped over to my cage.

'Happy New Year, Humphrey! You're looking handsome and healthy,' he told me.

Aldo is a true friend!

'And you the same,' I squeaked back.

'Who's your buddy?' Aldo glanced at Og. 'Hey, I know you. The frog from down the corridor. What are you doing here?'

'You don't want to know!' I squeaked.

Aldo turned back to me. 'Calm down, pal, I brought you something.' He reached into his pocket and unwrapped the most beautiful tiny tomato I've ever seen. I could have cried.

'Thanks, Aldo,' I squeaked as I tucked the treat in my cheek pouch.

'You're welcome, Humphrey.' Aldo looked over at Og again. 'Sorry, I don't know what frogs eat.'

'You don't want to know that either!' I assured him.

Aldo grabbed a paper bag and pulled a chair up close to me. 'May I join you for supper?' he asked.

He didn't need to ask. We'd shared many happy evenings while he ate his supper. I took a deep breath. Aldo gave off a pleasant smell of chalk dust and pine spray. He smelled the way I imagined a forest smells. Somewhere, WAY-WAY-WAY back in time, wild hamsters must have lived in forests, down in sweet, earthy piles of rotting leaves and fallen pine cones. Yeah, Aldo smelled like home!

'Mind if we have a little talk?' he asked.

Of course I didn't. I'd been trying to get old lumpy to talk all evening.

'I've got something to tell you, Humph. Remember how I gave my girlfriend Maria an engagement ring for Christmas? Well, I've got bigger news. On New Year's Day she and I ran off and got married!' He held up his left hand. A gold ring glittered on one finger.

'I hope you'll be HAPPY-HAPPY-HAPPY!' I squeaked with delight.

'Thanks, pal. I know I told you that you'd be at my wedding, but we decided to get hitched quietly. You understand?' he asked.

Naturally I squeaked, 'Yes.' After all, I'd helped them get together in the first place. And when I met Maria, she was as nice as Aldo.

'Yeah, I'm an old married man now. Really happy. But I've started thinking, Humphrey. I like this job, but it doesn't pay a whole lot.' Aldo paused to chew a bite of his sandwich. 'I'd like to have kids and a house and maybe raise a couple of hamsters of my own.'

Fine with me, as long as he didn't raise any frogs.

'I'd really love to have my evenings free to spend with my family. Pal, I've got to find a way to get a better job,' Aldo continued.

'You can do it!' I squeaked.

Aldo was quieter than usual as he finished his supper. I spun on my wheel to entertain him, but he was lost in thought. Finally, he folded up his bag.

'Guess I'm not good company tonight, Humphrey. I bet that frog makes better conversation than I do.'

'Fat chance,' I squeaked.

After Aldo had cleaned the room and left, I did some thinking. Personally, I believed that Aldo was already as fine a human as I've ever seen. I'd miss him if he worked somewhere else. But he was my friend, so if he wanted a better job, I wanted to help him.

I started jotting down ideas in my notebook and lost track of time. Later, I heard splashing. I'd almost forgotten about you know who next door.

'Hey, what's shaking, Og?' I called out to him. Maybe he'd thought about his behaviour and wanted to apologize for his bad manners.

There was no reply, just splish-splash-splish. Personally, the idea of being covered in water is disgusting to me. I prefer to groom myself the time-honoured way: using the tongue, teeth, paws and toenails. I thoroughly clean myself every day. The students in Room 26 love to watch me. At least they did before goggle-eyes came along.

Still, if I had to share a table with him, I thought I might TRY-TRY-TRY again to be friendly. 'Having a nice bath?' I asked.

There was no answer. Not even another splash. But there was another sound: the crickets. So they were alive after all!

Og *would* have to eat noisy food. My Nutri-Nibbles and Mighty Mealworms didn't make a sound until I crunched down on them. But the crickets – who I actually felt sorry for – made a funny singing noise: 'Chirrup, chirrup!' Apparently, they were nocturnal like me.

It was going to be a long night, with noisy crickets and a silent frog. I hopped on to my wheel and tried to spin my irritation away.

It didn't work.

> **The only way to have a friend is to be one.**
> Ralph Waldo Emerson.
> American poet and essayist

3 Sad-Mad-Bad

I'll tell you how the whole week went: TERRIBLE-TERRIBLE-TERRIBLE! It must have been National Frog Appreciation Week, because frogs were all we talked about in Room 26.

First, Mrs Brisbane taught everybody how to take care of Og. The students gathered around as she put on rubber gloves, picked up the container of insects and sprinkled a few into Og's tank. She didn't seem too happy about the crickets, which turned out to be quite large and ugly. The way they leaped around the tank, no wonder Og went 'Boing!'

'Did you see his tongue?' A.J. bellowed. 'It must be a foot long!'

'Oooh, he ate one!' Heidi squealed.

'Gross!' said Seth as Og's tongue grabbed the rest of the crickets.

'I want to pet him,' said Mandy. Before anyone could stop her, she slid the top off the tank, reached down and picked up the big lump of frog.

'No, Mandy!' said Mrs Brisbane. But it was too late.

'He peed on me!' Mandy shrieked, dropping Og back into his tank. Not that I blamed her. What unsqueakably bad manners! Is that any way for a classroom pet to act?

Seth jumped back, shaking his hands. 'Oooh!'

Gail giggled, of course, as did everyone else.

'Wash your hands with plenty of soap and hot water,' Mrs Brisbane told Mandy. To the rest of the class, she said, 'That's what frogs do when they're frightened. We must all be gentle with poor Og. If you have to touch him, you must wear gloves. Pick him up by the shoulder blades and never squeeze his stomach or you'll hurt him.'

She ordered my classmates back to their seats (not including Mandy, who was washing her hands). Then we had to learn more frog facts. They don't start out as cute, furry little babies like hamsters. NO-NO-NO! They start out as funny little tadpoles, and end up as big, lumpy frogs with bulgy eyes.

For some strange reason, everyone was fascinated with frogs, except Tabitha and me. She paid more attention to her teddy bear than to anything else in class.

I overheard Mandy complain to the other girls that Tabitha wasn't very friendly. 'I tried to get her to play at break, but she wasn't interested in anything besides that old bear. She's a big baby.'

Sayeh murmured, 'Maybe she's shy.' I was pleased that Sayeh had learned to speak up. But the other girls decided Tabitha was just unfriendly.

Like someone else who was new to Room 26.

·ö·

After so much frog talk, Mrs Brisbane moved on to the subject of poetry.

First, we read a scary poem about a tiger. We also read a poem about a bee, followed by a silly poem about a purple cow. Some poems rhyme and some don't. But there are a lot of rhyming words, like 'moon' and 'June', and 'cat' and 'rat'. (Funny that those last two words rhyme, isn't it?)

At night, while Og stared into space, I made lists of rhyming words in my notebook. Better than trying to talk to him, as he continued to give me the silent treatment.

Jumpy, bumpy, grumpy, lumpy. Funny that those words rhyme too!

After a few days spent reading poems, Mrs Brisbane said it was time for us to write our own poems. There were louder groans than on the first time she mentioned poetry. Mrs Brisbane held up her hand, which meant everybody had to be quiet.

'All this is in preparation for Valentine's Day, when our class will present a Poetry Festival for all the parents. Each of you will recite a poem you wrote or one you like.' There were no groans now. In fact, some of the students looked excited. Even Pay-Attention-Art Patel was paying attention.

Mrs Brisbane explained that our assignment was to write a poem about an animal, at least six lines long, with words that rhymed.

Mandy raised her hand and the teacher asked her to speak. 'My name rhymes with "candy cane",' Mandy proudly announced.

Mrs Brisbane smiled. 'That's right: "Mandy Payne" rhymes with "candy cane". Does anyone else have a rhyming name?'

'"Richie" rhymes with "itchy"!' A.J. blurted out.

'What?' asked Repeat-It-Please-Richie.

Words were flying through my brain. Humphrey-pumphrey-dumphrey-lumphrey.

'"Gail" rhymes with "hail"!' Heidi forgot to raise her hand again.

'And "fail",' Kirk muttered.

'I-Heard-That-Kirk Chen,' said Mrs Brisbane.

'Well, "Kirk" rhymes with "jerk",' said Heidi, who was always ready to defend her best friend Gail.

'Please, no more,' Mrs Brisbane said firmly.

'"Kirk" also rhymes with "work". So let's get back to work.'

I never saw my classmates work so hard before. Richie chewed on his pencil, Seth jiggled his leg, Heidi erased more than she wrote, Kirk scratched his head and Miranda wrote and wrote and wrote. Then she stopped writing and raised her hand.

'Mrs Brisbane, can you think of anything that rhymes with "hamster"?' she asked.

'Let's throw that one out to the class,' said the teacher. 'Anyone?'

Leave it to Golden Miranda to ask such a good question. It got everybody thinking, because the room was so quiet you could have heard a pencil drop. Two pencils did drop, in fact.

'How about "gangster"?' a voice called out.

'Raise-Your-Hand-Heidi.' Mrs Brisbane walked to the blackboard. 'How about that, class? Does "HAMster" rhyme with "GANGster"?'

She wrote the words on the blackboard and repeated them. 'Hear that? They don't have quite the same sound, do they?'

Well, I should hope not! Gangsters are bad guys and I am definitely a good guy.

'Maybe you'd better find another word to rhyme,' the teacher instructed.

'Try "Humphrey"!' I squeaked in encouragement. There had to be something that rhymed.

'Try "frog"!' shouted A.J.

'Lower-Your-Voice-A.J.,' Mrs Brisbane reminded him.

'And raise your hand,' added Heidi.

Mrs Brisbane shook her head, then began to write words on the board as my classmates shouted them out. Dog, fog, log, slog, clog and more.

Nothing rhymed with 'hamster', but everything rhymed with 'frog'. How depressing! I wondered how many words rhyme with 'sad'? Like 'mad' and 'bad'.

⚬

After break, it was Miranda's turn to clean my cage. She always does an extra-good job of cleaning my potty corner and changing my water and bedding. And she always has a special treat for me, like a piece of cauliflower. Yum.

'Sorry, Humphrey, I tried to write a poem about you,' she told me. 'I think I'm going to have to write about Clem instead.'

Clem was Miranda's dog, the one who tried to eat me when I stayed at her house. How Golden Miranda could put up with Clem was beyond me.

That night, I wrote my very first poem ever. I asked Og if he wanted to hear it. His silence wasn't too encouraging, but I decided to read it anyway.

When Ms Mac left me for Brazil.
She made me SAD–SAD–SAD.
When Clem the dog was mean to me.
I felt real MAD–MAD–MAD.
Now Og's moved in and he has got me
Feeling BAD–BAD–BAD.
In fact. this is the worst week
I ever HAD–HAD–HAD!

I waited to hear Og applaud or at least give me a grudging 'Boing'. I heard only silence. When I glanced over at my neighbour, he was grinning from ear to ear. Or he would have been if he had ears. Somehow, his smile didn't cheer me up at all.

·ö·

I felt better the following day, though, because it was Friday. That meant I would get a little break from Room 26 and the green and grumpy lump. Every weekend a different student took me home, and I'd had many wonderful adventures with my classmates and their families. I'd even gone home with Mr Morales the headmaster!

This week, I was going home with Wait-For-The-Bell-Garth Tugwell. He'd wanted to take me home for a long time.

'Can I take Og home, too?' asked Garth.

'I think Og can stay here,' Mrs Brisbane

answered. 'Frogs don't need to eat every day, except when they're young.'

Funny, I didn't feel quite so sad-mad-bad any more.

·̇ȯ·̇

'Can't your mum pick us up?' A.J. asked Garth after school.

I couldn't see him, but I could hear him as we waited outside for the bus. I had a blanket over my cage because it was cold outside. I didn't mind, though, as long as I was FAR-FAR-FAR away from Og. (Who hadn't even tried to say 'goodbye' to me.)

'My dad said not to bother her. She's been ill,' said Garth. 'Couldn't your mum pick us up?'

'I wish.' A.J. sighed. 'She has to pick up my sister from kindergarten and put the baby down for a nap.'

'Did you tell your parents about Bean?' asked Garth.

At least I thought he said 'Bean'. Things sounded a little muffled under the blanket.

'Nah,' said A.J. 'Last time I said somebody was picking on me, my dad signed me up for boxing lessons. I hated people punching me. It was worse than being picked on.'

I tried to sort out what A.J. meant about getting picked on. By a bean? By a boxing bean? I didn't have time to figure it out before the bus arrived.

'Here goes,' said Garth, lifting my cage. 'Let's stick together, no matter what.'

'OK. Be sure to sit in front by Miss Victoria,' whispered A.J. 'That's the safest.'

By the shuffling and scuffling sounds, I could tell that we were on the bus. Luckily, a corner of the blanket slipped down and I could see Miss Victoria, the bus driver, glancing over her shoulder.

'Keep moving, guys,' she said in a firm voice. 'Whoa, ladies, one of you has to go. Can't have three in a seat.' Three first-year girls were huddled together in the seat right behind the bus driver. 'We're not moving until one of you goes. You move, Beth.'

The girl on the end timidly got up and started down the aisle, nervously looking back at her friends.

'Keep going, folks,' Miss Victoria snapped.

Suddenly – BOOM! The girl named Beth fell down flat on the floor right in front of us. Her books slid around the floor in all directions.

The bus was quiet as Beth lay there, until somebody said, 'Hey, clumsy, you dropped something!' That was followed by a nasty snigger.

'You tripped her,' said A.J. in a voice not quite as loud as usual.

'Says you, A.J.! What do those letters stand for anyway? Awful Jerk?'

I crawled over to the side of the cage to see who was speaking. He was BIG-BIG-BIG for a kid. He had spiky hair and a scowl on his face.

As Garth and A.J. bent over to help Beth pick up her books, Miss Victoria called to the back of the bus.

'Garth and A.J., if you don't sit down so I can get moving, I'm going to report you two.'

'Yeah, Garth Bugwart, sit down,' the big kid sneered.

'I'm going to tell,' Beth said softly.

'Don't!' A.J. whispered back. 'Bean will only get worse.'

So this was the scary Bean they were talking about!

Beth slid into a seat with all her books. Just as A.J. stepped forward, Bean stuck his leg into the aisle. So that's how he had tripped her! After A.J. managed to step over it, Garth and I (in my cage) were standing right next to Mr Nasty.

'What's in the cage, Bugface? Your lunch?' He snorted a few times, but no one else on the bus laughed. 'Or is that your girlfriend?'

That did it! I was fighting mad. Somebody had to squeak up to this fellow. 'For your information, I am a male Golden Hamster. And you are one MEAN BEAN!'

'Anybody got a mousetrap?' Bean snarled.

'Why aren't you guys in your seats?' Miss Victoria yelled from the front of the bus. 'I'm reporting you, Garth and A.J.!'

Garth slid into a seat next to A.J. I was about to give Miss Victoria a piece of my mind when the bus lurched forward and I had to hold on to my cage for dear life. I was sorry I'd eaten those Nutri-Nibbles just before we left.

All week, I'd been looking forward to going home with Garth. Now I wasn't sure I'd ever make it there!

Friendship is one mind in two bodies.
Mencius. Chinese philosopher

I am a male Golden Hamster ✓

I am NOT: lunch ✗
a rat ✗
a mouse ✗
a ham ✗
a hammer ✗
an 'it' ✗

4 Mean Bean

A.J.'s stop was before Garth's. 'Come on over tomorrow,' Garth told his friend. As soon as A.J. left, Garth moved up to the front of the bus to get away from Bean.

'What part of "sit down" don't you understand, Garth?' Miss Victoria sounded pretty irritated.

'Sorry. The cage wouldn't fit on the seat,' he said.

'What on earth is in there, anyway?'

Before Garth could answer, the bus stopped in front of his house. He pulled the blanket down around my cage and hurried down the steps.

Mrs Tugwell was waiting in the doorway of the house. She had wavy brown hair like her son. She had glasses and freckles like her son too. She helped him set my cage up on the living-room table. Garth's little brother Andy raced into the room.

He had wavy brown hair, glasses and freckles too. 'Mine!' he shouted.

'Nope. He's mine. At least for the weekend,' said Garth.

'Tell Andy about Humphrey,' Garth's mum said.

'He's a hamster. And you have to be nice to him,' Garth explained.

He got that right!

'I like ham,' said Andy, rubbing his stomach. 'Yum-yum!'

I hopped on to my wheel to show Andy that a hamster wasn't anything like a ham.

'Wheee! Ham go round!' said Andy.

Garth's mother brought in a plate of peanut butter and crackers. Ooh, that smelled good!

'How was school?' she asked.

'OK,' said Garth. 'But Mum, could you say something to Bean's mum? He's mean to everybody on the bus.'

'Martin Bean?' Garth's mum sounded surprised. 'Why, he's always polite when I see him.'

'Well, he's not polite any other time,' Garth explained. 'He tripped a girl on the bus and called everybody names.'

'That doesn't sound like Martin. What did the bus driver do?'

'Nothing,' Garth answered.

'Well, I think she should be the one to work things out,' said Mrs Tugwell.

'But you're friends with Mrs Bean!'

'I probably won't be if I complain about her son. Maybe if you were friendlier to him, he'd act nicer.'

'Mum . . .' Garth moaned.

'It's worth a try,' his mum suggested.

I had to squeak up. 'He's the Meanest Bean I've ever seen!'

'Goodness, what's the matter with Humphrey?' asked Mrs Tugwell.

'Maybe he doesn't like Marty either,' Garth muttered. He's one smart fellow.

Shortly after Mr Tugwell came home, Natalie arrived. She was the babysitter, but I didn't see any babies around for her to sit on. Garth wasn't a baby, Andy wasn't a baby and certainly I was no baby.

Natalie had black hair and wore a black shirt, black trousers and black shoes. She had glasses with black frames. Her lips were bright red.

'Order a pizza,' said Garth's dad, handing Natalie some money. 'I got some videos for the guys.'

'OK,' said Natalie. 'Mind if I do some homework?'

'As long as you get the boys into bed at nine,' Mrs Tugwell agreed.

Natalie glanced at my cage. 'What about the rat?'

I felt quite discouraged. I'd already been called a mouse and a ham that day.

'He's a hammer!' Andy yelled.

'Oh, a hamster. How cute,' said Natalie, leaning in towards my cage. 'Hi there, big boy.'

Whew! After a miserable week and a rough ride home, I suddenly felt a whole lot better.

·ö·

Later, the boys ate pizza and watched videos while Natalie read from a big thick book.

'What's that?' asked Andy, leaning over her shoulder. 'How come it doesn't have any pictures?'

'College books don't have pictures.'

Andy wrinkled his nose. 'What's college?'

Natalie sighed. 'After you go to secondary school and pass your exams, if you want a good job like a doctor or a lawyer or a teacher, you have to go to college.'

'I know that,' Garth piped up. 'City College is right down the street. Mum took classes there last year.'

'That's where I go,' said Natalie. 'I'm studying psychology.' The way she said it, that big word sounded like 'sigh-coll-eh-gee'. But the word on her book was spelled 'Psychology'. I wrote it down in my notebook later. (I hope that word is never in a spelling test!)

'In psychology, you find out what's inside people's heads.' The babysitter reached for Andy's head.

'Ooey-gooey brains,' said Garth.

'Don't go into my head!' screamed Andy, leaping off the sofa.

Natalie laughed. 'Not like that. Psychology teaches you how people think. Do you know what I'm thinking?'

Andy shook his head.

'I'm thinking it's time for bed,' Natalie said. 'Nine o'clock.'

The boys both groaned. 'Not yet,' Garth protested.

Andy folded his arms. 'You can't make me!' he said firmly.

Surprisingly, Natalie sat back and smiled. 'I suppose you're right. I can't make you.'

Andy's eyes practically bugged out of his head. 'Huh?'

'Why don't you put on another video? We can stay up till your parents get back,' the babysitter continued. 'It'll be fun!'

'Yes!' Garth exclaimed as he and his brother gleefully high-fived each other.

But I was a little confused. Hadn't Mrs Tugwell told her to get the boys into bed at nine? I was sure that Natalie had lost her mind.

Garth settled back on the sofa, but after a minute

his smile disappeared. 'When do you think Mum and Dad will be back?'

Natalie shrugged her shoulders. 'They didn't say.'

'Won't they be upset if we're still up?'

'I suppose we'll find out, won't we?' Natalie answered with a mischievous grin.

Andy looked worried. 'They'll be cross if we're not in bed.'

'So?' said Natalie. 'We still have time to watch more TV.'

Garth stood up and yawned loudly. 'I'm kind of tired.'

'Me too,' said Andy, stretching his arms.

Natalie smiled. 'Well, if you really think so, OK. You two get ready for bed and I'll be up in a minute.'

As the brothers raced upstairs, Natalie chuckled to herself, then leaned in towards my cage.

'And that, Humphrey Hamster, is what is called "reverse psychology". You get people to do what you want by telling them to do the opposite.'

Reverse psychology. (Remember, it's pronounced sigh-coll-er-gee.) So that's how people's minds work. Just tell them to do the opposite of what you want them to do.

You can really learn a lot at college.

You can learn a lot from a good babysitter too.

The next afternoon, A.J. came over to Garth's house to play. Mrs Tugwell took Andy out to buy new shoes. Mr Tugwell was paying bills in the kitchen. The boys were alone with me in the living room.

'Humphrey needs some exercise,' said A.J. 'Let's take him out.'

'OK. You can watch him while I clean his cage.'

A.J. gently took me out while Garth put on gloves and began to clean my cage. Both boys chuckled when Garth got to my potty corner – everyone does – but he did a good job of cleaning it. While he worked, they talked.

'Any chance your dad can drive us on Monday morning?' asked Garth.

A.J. shook his head as he gently petted me. 'He has to leave for work really early. How about your dad?'

Garth shook his head. 'He always talks about how he had to walk to school and how lucky I am to ride on a bus.'

'I know,' A.J. sighed and put me down on the table.

'Watch it!' said Garth. He set up a row of big tall books all around the edge of the table. 'We don't want Humphrey to get away.'

'Maybe he'll be sick on Monday,' Garth suggested.

'Are you kidding? He's the healthiest guy at school. Man, if he wasn't so big, I'd really give it to him,' said A.J., making a fist.

'Me too,' Garth agreed.

It wasn't hard to work out that they were talking about big mean Marty Bean.

'I don't know why Miss Victoria always takes his side,' Garth said after a while.

'He knows how not to get caught.'

The boys were silent again until Garth said, 'Miranda was getting a drink at the fountain at break, and he came up and pushed her out of the way.'

The thought of someone pushing Golden Miranda, an almost perfect human, really ruffled my fur.

'Did she tell?' asked A.J.

'Yeah. He said he didn't do it,' Garth explained. 'Said he wasn't anywhere near her. He said Kirk did it. Kirk almost got into trouble, so Miranda said it was all a mistake to get Kirk off the hook.'

'Kirk the Jerk. That's what Bean calls him,' said Garth. 'He's got a name for everybody. That's why he doesn't have any friends.'

He stepped back and pulled off his rubber gloves. 'I think that's one clean cage.'

'Great,' I squeaked. 'But what are we going to do about Bean?'

'Bean's a pretty funny name,' A.J. said with a chuckle. 'Bean brain.'

'Bean breath,' said Garth.

The boys started laughing.

'Bean bag!'

'Bean jeans!'

'Green Bean!'

'Mean Bean! Hey – that rhymes! Mean green Bean!'

Mrs Brisbane would be proud to hear them rhyming! I liked hearing them laugh. However, I was worried. Bean had said something about a mousetrap. The mere mention of those contraptions makes me shiver and quiver. And I didn't want to see anybody get tripped or pushed again.

'Ready to go back in, Humphrey-Dumpty?' asked Garth.

'YES!' I squeaked, which for some reason made the boys howl with laughter again.

Once I was back in the cage, the boys went up to play in Garth's room. That gave me time to think. Here were Garth and A.J., really good friends. They were nice to each other and stuck together. Marty Bean wasn't friendly to anybody and he didn't have any friends.

All my classmates liked Og, but when I offered

to be his friend, he leaped at me in a very rude way. The business of friendship is not as easy as it sounds, I figured, just before dozing off for a long afternoon nap.

It was nice at Garth's house that weekend. The announcer on TV said it was COLD-COLD-COLD outside, so the Tugwells stayed inside. The family popped popcorn – did that smell good! And they watched TV and snuggled on the sofa. As happy as I should have been, I worried about Monday's bus ride. What I needed was a Plan. And maybe a little psychology.

'Are you sure the little fellow won't catch cold?' asked Mrs Tugwell when Garth was ready to leave for school on Monday.

'He's got a fur coat. And I'll cover him,' Garth assured her. I was plunged into total darkness as he threw a blanket over the cage.

'Bye, Ham!' shouted Andy.

'Bye, Andy!' I squeaked back. After all, a 'ham' isn't the worst thing that a person can call you.

Soon, I heard the squeal of the bus's brakes as it stopped in front of the Tugwells' house.

'All aboard!' I heard Miss Victoria say. 'Find a seat.'

'This cage is too big. Can't I sit up here?' asked Garth.

'Do you see any empty seats up here?' the bus driver replied. 'Get moving and keep moving.'

I was already queasy just thinking about Bean. As Garth walked towards the back of the bus, looking for an empty seat, my cage swayed back and forth like a ship on a rough sea, which didn't help my stomach at all. Once we sat down, the bus started rolling. At the next corner, it abruptly stopped and I slid across the floor of my cage. Ouch!

'All aboard!' I heard Miss Victoria say. 'Find a seat, A.J.'

A.J. walked back to our seat. 'Move over,' he told Garth.

'I have to sit on the aisle,' Garth replied. 'The cage won't fit in the seat.'

A.J. crawled over Garth so that he was close to the window. As he did, he bent down and whispered, 'Told you he'd be here. He's always here.'

As the bus lurched forward, my cage wobbled enough for the blanket to part, so I could see a little. And what I saw was most unpleasant: Marty Bean sitting right next to us.

'Hey, Garth, is that your face or did somebody throw up on you?' I could see the smirk on his face as he leaned in close, mere inches from my cage.

'Is that a cage, Bugwart, or is it your handbag?'

Bean asked. He hooted at his own joke even though it wasn't funny.

It may have been cold outside, but I was getting pretty hot. Og might be unfriendly, but this Bean was even worse. I hadn't thought of Og all weekend. Now it came back to me: the green skin, the repulsive grin, and the way he had leaped up and scared me. I had taken it from the frog, but I wasn't going to take it from this big bully.

This was the time to act!

I quickly opened the lock-that-doesn't-lock and took a deep breath before leaping on to Martin Bean's leg. 'Stop being mean, Bean!' I yelled at the top of my voice. It may have sounded like squeaking to him, but I made my point.

'Eeek!' Marty shouted. 'It's on me! A mouse!' He threw his hands up in the air and screamed as I ran in circles on his leg. 'Help me, somebody! Help!'

The faces around me were a blur and I was getting dizzy. As Marty continued to scream, the other kids began to laugh, softly at first, then louder and louder.

'He's only a little hamster,' I heard Garth say as he scooped me up in his hands. 'He wouldn't hurt a flea.'

I like being called a 'he' a lot more than being called an 'it'.

'It tried to bite me!' Marty exclaimed. Everybody

on the bus, including Beth and her first-year friends, laughed.

'What is going on back there, Martin?' Miss Victoria called out as she slammed on the brakes.

'They – they threw a big rat on me!' He was almost in tears. 'A giant rat!'

'I think you'd better come up and sit behind me,' the bus driver said. 'Now!' She made the girls in the seat behind her move as Marty shuffled to the front of the bus.

Garth put me back in my cage.

'Thanks, Humphrey,' he whispered. 'I don't know how you got out, but I'm really glad you did.'

'Always happy to help out a pal,' I squeaked.

The rest of the ride was uneventful. When Miss Victoria stopped the bus in front of Longfellow School, she made an announcement. 'This was the quietest ride we've ever had. From now on, Martin Bean, I'm assigning you the front seat. Permanently.'

Marty didn't argue. He was in too much of a hurry to get off the bus. He could probably hear all the rest of the bus passengers – including me – shouting, 'Hooray!'

> **No enemy can match a friend.**
> Jonathan Swift. Irish author

5 Rhyme Time

I felt pretty proud of myself after the bus ride. Once I was back in Room 26, I looked over at my pop-eyed neighbour.

'Morning, Og,' I squeaked to him, hoping that after the long, lonely weekend he might be in a friendlier frame of mind. He responded to my greeting with dead silence and a grim grin. Or maybe he couldn't see me, because there was a huge piece of paper taped to the front of his glass box.

And something about that note must have been pretty funny, because all my classmates were laughing. Hard.

'All right, what's so funny?' asked Mrs Brisbane.

'Og!' said Gail. She was giggling so hard I was afraid she'd get the hiccups again.

Mrs Brisbane ripped the paper off the tank and

read it. 'Help! I'm a prince who's been turned into a frog. Kiss me quick!'

Somebody made loud smacking sounds, which made everyone laugh even louder. Mrs Brisbane looked up from the paper. 'I-Heard-That-Kirk. Are you volunteering to kiss Og?'

It was a pretty disgusting thought to me, but everyone else laughed.

'I think it has to be a girl,' said Kirk.

Mrs Brisbane folded up the paper. 'Thank you for our joke of the day. You can Stop-Giggling-Gail. Now, let's all calm down and get to work. I'm anxious to hear the poems you've written, but let's get our spelling test out of the way first. Please take out a pencil and a piece of paper.'

Whoops! I'd done a lot of thinking over the weekend. Something I hadn't thought about was our spelling test. Mrs Brisbane and my classmates don't know that I usually slip into my sleeping house with my notebook and pencil and take the tests, too. I still hadn't got 100 per cent, like Sayeh. I hoped I would some day.

This would not be the day.

I did all right with 'market', 'jewel' and 'pound'. But 'accommodate'? Did Mrs Brisbane really think anyone except Sayeh would get that right? It looks like they threw in some extra letters left over from another word!

Next, it was time for the poems. 'Kirk, you seem to want to be the centre of attention this morning. You can go first.'

Kirk jumped up and said, 'I've got to write mine on the board.'

Mrs Brisbane told him to go ahead. When he was finished, he read it aloud.

'It's called 'Frog'. Here goes:

> **Funny**
> **Ribbits**
> **Oily**
> **Green**.
> That's a **frog**.
> Take away the funny ribbits
> You've got Og?!'

Mrs Brisbane smiled and nodded her head. 'Well done, Kirk. Very clever. What do you think, class?'

'Does that say "oily"?' asked Repeat-It-Please-Richie. 'Frogs aren't oily.'

Kirk wrinkled his nose. 'Well, he looks oily, even if he isn't. Besides, I need an O word to spell "frog".'

Mrs Brisbane asked the class to help Kirk out with another O word. I decided to squeak up.

'Obnoxious! Offensive!' I yelled. I almost said, 'Unfriendly,' but it doesn't begin with an O.

No one seemed to hear me. Sometimes I wish I had a big booming voice like A.J.'s.

'"Honest"?' asked Seth, jumping up out of his seat.

'Sit-Still-Seth. That's a good guess, but "honest" starts with a silent H.' Mrs Brisbane wrote the word on the board. Silent H – not fair! I'll have to watch out for that one.

'How about "odd"?' suggested Art.

'What do you think, class? Do some people think frogs are odd?'

Some students nodded their heads. Nobody nodded harder than me.

'What do you think?' the teacher asked Kirk.

'Maybe "oddball" fits him better,' Kirk said, smiling. Everybody seemed to like the answer and I was not about to disagree.

I glanced over at Og to see what he thought. 'Boing,' he twanged. Everybody laughed, even Mrs Brisbane.

'Oh, Og, you are so funny,' she said.

Oddball, yes. Funny, no. In my humble opinion.

Heidi waved her hand in the air. 'Og doesn't say "ribbit". He goes "boing".'

'R is for "boing"? Heidi, that makes "roing".' Kirk looked very pleased with himself.

Heidi frowned. 'That's not what I meant.'

'That's enough on that one, Kirk. Why don't you work on it a little more?' said Mrs Brisbane. She called for another volunteer. This time Heidi actually remembered to raise her hand. When the teacher called on her, she stood up and read her poem.

> I met a little frog
> And said. 'How do you do?
> My name is Hopper.
> Is that your name too?'
> He croaked. 'My name is Leaper.
> That's what I do all day.'
> But when I tried to pick him up.
> Leaper ran away.

'Nicely done, Heidi,' said Mrs Brisbane. 'Good rhyming. It's a good idea to use your own name. Anyone else?'

No hands were raised this time.

'How about you, Tabitha?' asked the teacher. 'What did you write?'

Tabitha looked SCARED-SCARED-SCARED.

Mrs Brisbane put on her friendliest smile. 'Don't be afraid. We won't bite, will we, class?'

Most of the kids smiled and shook their heads. Kirk growled like a lion, just to be funny, but I couldn't tell if Tabitha noticed.

Slowly, she stood up and picked up her paper. In a soft voice, she read her poem like it was one sentence, really fast, like this:

'*People-think-bears-are-mean-but-they've-never-seen-Smiley. He-doesn't-growl-or-make-you-sad-he-wouldn't-ever-be-bad-Smiley. I-don't-care-what-people-say-he-helps-me-get-through-the-day-Smiley.*'

Tabitha quickly sat down and stared at her table.

'Thank you, Tabitha. That's a lovely poem about a bear. And I liked the rhymes,' said Mrs Brisbane.

I saw Tabitha reach into her pocket and pat her teddy bear.

I also saw Mandy look over at Heidi and roll her eyes. I could even read her lips as she mouthed the word 'baby'.

'Any volunteers?' asked the teacher. 'Garth?' Garth stood up to read his poem.

> Roses are red.
> Frogs are cool.
> Now we've got one
> Here at school.

He folded up his paper. 'That's it.'

Mrs Brisbane reminded Garth that the poems were supposed to have at least six lines and that his poem had four.

Personally, I was in shock.

'Frogs are *cool*'? What kind of a poem is that? After I helped him and A.J. with Mean Bean, Garth wrote 'Frogs are cool'?

We didn't have time for any more poems because the bell rang for break and my classmates raced to get their coats and gloves.

Tabitha took her time, waiting to see that no one was watching, and secretly stashed her bear in her pocket. Sayeh stayed behind too, and approached her.

'I liked your poem. Is Smiley your bear's name?' she asked.

Tabitha nodded, but she didn't say anything. She didn't know how shy Sayeh was or how hard it was for her to come up and talk like that. But I knew.

'He's nice,' said Sayeh. 'Are you coming out to break?'

Tabitha nodded again. Sayeh waited, but when Tabitha didn't budge, she said, 'See you outside,' and hurried to the cloakroom with her head down, looking embarrassed.

I've got to admit, Speak-Up-Sayeh is a favourite friend of mine. To see Tabitha treat her that way made me MAD-MAD-MAD. She was about as friendly as a frog!

The new girl waited until everyone else had left the room before rising to get her coat.

Later, after the students left for the day, Miss Loomis came into Room 26, all bundled up in her coat, hat and gloves.

'Hi, Sue. I'm ready when you are.' She walked over to Og's cage. 'How's your star pupil doing?'

'Fine. He and Humphrey seem to get along all right. At least they don't disturb each other,' said Mrs Brisbane.

Don't disturb each other? I was pretty disturbed when Og leaped at me!

Mrs Brisbane put on her coat. 'Let's stop for coffee to warm us up on the way home.'

'Sounds great,' Miss Loomis answered. 'I can't thank you enough for giving me a lift.'

'What are friends for?' asked Mrs Brisbane.

After they left, I felt as gloomy as the sky looked. Spinning my wheel warmed my fur up, but it didn't make me feel any warmer inside. What are friends for? For fun and talking and helping and sharing. Right?

'Hey, Og!' I called out, peering through the bars of my cage at his glass house. 'I hope you've been paying attention here in Room 26.'

I waited a few seconds to allow him to answer, which he didn't, of course. 'I hope you've seen what good friends the kids are. I mean, like Garth and A.J., the way they stick together. And Heidi and Gail, the way they like to giggle. Sayeh and Miranda are pals. Art and Richie, too. Wouldn't it be nice to have fun friends like them?'

I didn't actually expect an answer, of course, but

this time I did get something: splashing. Splish-splash-splish. At least I knew Og was alive. Maybe he was even listening. I kept going. 'Even if we can't actually talk to each other, we could – I don't know – have jumping contests.' Suddenly, I had all kinds of ideas. 'We could sing together. Or make funny faces at each other. Maybe you could teach me how to go "boing".'

'Boing!'

I almost fainted. Was he answering me?

'Boing,' I said, though I didn't sound much like a frog. 'Boing to you, Og!'

'Boing-boing!' said Og.

'Yeah ... boing!' I replied. My heart was thumping quite loudly. Were we actually having a conversation? 'Uh ... so what else is new?' I continued.

I waited, but there was no answer. 'Og?' I called out. 'Og, answer me!'

Silence. This was one frustrating frog. I tried again, but there were no more boings. Not even a splash. The room was silent as a tomb. That's about as quiet as it can get.

Somehow, it felt even worse to think that Og tried to talk to me and gave up. Still, Sayeh had learned a brand-new language when she came to this country. Maybe Og and I could learn to understand each other. I returned to my wheel and started spinning as fast as I could. I spun until it was almost dark.

At last, the door swung open and the lights came on.

'I have arrived!' Aldo announced, waving his broom. 'No applause, please.'

'HELLO-HELLO-HELLO!' I shouted. I was never so glad to see anybody in my life.

Aldo hurried towards my cage, rubbing his arms.

'Hey, it's cold in here. They turn the heat down at night to save money, but it's freezing outside. And it's almost freezing in here,' said Aldo. He glanced at Og's cage. 'Hey, Og, how's the world treating you?'

When Og didn't answer him, Aldo turned back to me. 'He's the strong, silent type, I suppose. Say, Humph, old pal, I've been thinking. About that idea of getting a better job, you know? Maria thinks I should go back to school.'

I tried to imagine Aldo sitting at a little table all day with Miranda, Richie and Seth. I didn't think his legs would fit.

'I could go to college during the day and still work here at night.'

College! I hoped they had bigger chairs there.

Aldo pulled up a chair so we were practically whisker to whisker. 'See, I went to college for a year. When my dad died, I quit because I needed to make money. I thought I'd go back, but I never did.'

'It's never too late,' I squeaked.

Aldo shook his head. 'I'm not a kid any more.' He reached into his pocket. 'Maria got me this application for City College, but I don't know.'

City College! That's where Natalie the babysitter went! She said that's where people go to become doctors and lawyers and teachers. That's where people go to study things like psychology and get good jobs.

'GO-GO-GO!' I said, hopping up and down.

'Maria thinks I'm clever enough,' said Aldo. 'I just don't know if I can handle all that studying.' He sighed and rose from his chair.

'Guess I'd better get this room cleaned or I won't have a job at all.' Aldo tucked the application back into his pocket. 'First, I'm going to go and turn up the heat.'

Good old Aldo. He was a thoughtful fellow. And a smart fellow, too. I hoped his wife could talk him into going back to school.

I wasn't sure I could do it all by myself. And I was pretty sure Og wouldn't be any help at all.

> **One of the most beautiful qualities of true friendship is to understand and to be understood.**
> Seneca, Roman playwright

6 Crabby Abby

The next morning, Kirk hurried from the cloakroom and stuck a big piece of paper on my cage. It almost blocked my view of Og, which was not a bad thing.

Once the other students had settled in their seats, they started giggling and pointing, led by Gail, of course. Mrs Brisbane looked puzzled until she glanced over at my cage. The sign read: HELP! I'M BEING HELD PRISONER IN ROOM 26!

'And who is responsible for this, as if I didn't know?' she asked.

Kirk rose and took a bow as everyone applauded. I joined in, though I was the only one who knew I could never be a prisoner with my lock-that-doesn't-lock.

'Let's all sit down now,' said Mrs Brisbane. 'And get back to poetry.'

Somebody made a very, very rude noise and Mrs Brisbane did not like that one little bit. 'I-Heard-That-Kirk. And I don't ever want to hear it again.'

·ö·

During the rest of the week, we heard a lot more animal poems. Most of them were about frogs. One was about a dog (Miranda's). Sayeh wrote about a beautiful bird called a dove. ('Dove' rhymes with 'love.')

Nobody wrote about hamsters.

Aldo didn't mention City College again. And Tabitha still didn't talk to anybody except Smiley.

I was looking forward to a change of scenery by the end of the week. A relaxing getaway to one of my classmates' cosy homes. One with plenty of heat and no frogs.

·ö·

On Friday, Mrs Brisbane said, 'I can't remember – who asked me about taking Humphrey home this weekend?' Miranda's hand shot up.

'Yes, Miranda. I got the note from your father. That will be fine.'

I let out a little 'Eek!' I don't think anyone heard me. Everyone knows that I have a special place in my hamster heart for Miranda. After all, her name is Golden and I am a Golden Hamster. We both have lovely golden hair.

But I have a terrible fear of her dog Clem. I barely escaped a terrible fate the last time I went home with her, but could I do it again?

Then it hit me. 'Wait a second! Did you say "father"?' I squeaked. Because when I went home with Miranda before, there was only her mum. And the dog, of course. And Fanny the fish.

Mrs Brisbane chuckled. 'I think Humphrey approves.'

I puzzled over this all afternoon. Sure enough, at the end of the day, a tall man called Mr Golden arrived to pick up his daughter. At least I wouldn't be riding on the bus with Marty Bean – that was a break! Miranda, thoughtful as ever, threw a warm blanket over my cage. As they carried me out, Mrs Brisbane picked up Og's cage.

'I thought you said Og stayed here at weekends,' said Miranda.

Mrs Brisbane chuckled. 'It's a surprise for my husband. He always enjoys Humphrey, so I thought he'd get a kick out of having Og for the weekend.'

I felt COLD-COLD-COLD and we were still inside! I thought the Brisbanes were my best friends of all. Were they ready to replace me with a frog?

Once we were in the car, I didn't have time to

worry about the Brisbanes. I was too worried about facing Clem again. I could practically see his sloppy tongue and drippy nose and smell that bad breath waiting for me up in Miranda's flat.

What a shock it was when the car pulled up in front of a house, not a block of flats. 'Here we are, Humphrey,' Miranda announced. 'You've seen my mum's place, but this weekend we're staying at my dad's place.'

A nice lady Miranda called 'Amy' met us at the door.

'Hi, honey,' said Mr Golden, kissing Amy on the cheek. 'Meet Humphrey the hamster.'

'Cute,' Amy replied. 'I think he should stay in the girls' room.'

'What about the living room?' asked Miranda. 'Or the dining-room table?'

'I think he'd get in the way,' Mr Golden said. 'Let's go to your room.'

Miranda's room in the flat had a bed, a desk, a fish tank and stars on the ceiling. Her room in this house had two beds, a dresser, a desk and no stars. Everything in this room was pink, from the walls to the bedspreads to the carpet on the floor. A girl about Miranda's age was sprawled across one bed, reading a magazine.

'What's THAT?' she asked in an unpleasant voice.

'Humphrey. He's our class hamster,' Miranda explained.

'Well, he's not staying in my room,' the girl stated firmly.

'It's Miranda's room too, Abby,' Amy said as she came through the door behind us. 'Put Humphrey on the desk.'

Miranda thoughtfully opened my cage to straighten out my ladder and my water bottle, which had slid around during the drive.

'Mum, I have to do homework on that desk,' said Abby, sitting up.

Huh? Amy was Abby's mum and she was married to Miranda's dad? Things were quite confusing.

'OK, we'll put his cage on the floor,' said Amy.

I heard a baby crying in another room. 'I've got to see what Ben wants,' she said. Mr Golden followed her and Abby got up to close the door.

'He stays on your side of the room,' Abby told Miranda. 'And don't forget, no crossing the line.'

Abby took her foot and dragged it in a straight line across the middle of the pink carpet. 'No crossing the line. Ever.'

Miranda sighed. 'I know. You tell me every time I'm here.'

'Sometimes you forget. And don't touch anything of mine.'

'I never do,' Miranda countered.

'You used my hair slide last time,' said Abby.

'It was a mistake! It looks exactly like mine!' Good for Miranda for standing up for herself! 'I didn't complain when you borrowed my book without asking.'

Abby plopped back on to the bed again and thumbed through her magazine. 'Just don't cross the line,' she muttered.

I hopped on my wheel for a spin. Sometimes it cheers people up to watch me spinning. Abby was not one of those people. She glared at me. 'Don't tell me it makes a noise,' she said nastily. 'Can't you stop it?'

'Humphrey is not an "it". He's a "he",' said Miranda. I love that girl! 'You could read in the living room,' she suggested.

'I was here first.' Abby suddenly slammed down her magazine and stood up. 'OK, anything to get away from you.'

After she left, Miranda leaned down close to my cage. 'I was hoping she'd like you, Humphrey. She certainly doesn't like me. It's not my fault my dad married her mum. It's not my fault she has to share her room with me every other weekend.' She sighed. 'I've tried to be friends with her, but it's no use. She's a wicked stepsister, like in Cinderella.'

Miranda looked SAD-SAD-SAD, so I leaped

up on my ladder and hung from it by one paw to cheer her up.

She smiled, so I leaped on to my tree and began swinging from branch to branch, like that Tarzan guy I saw on TV. That made Miranda laugh.

Abby returned with a sour expression on her face. I must have looked that way the day somebody in Room 26 (I'm still trying to work out who) slipped me a slice of lemon.

'Mum wants us to help make supper. She's got to feed the baby.'

She disappeared as quickly as she had appeared.

'See you, Humphrey,' Miranda whispered. 'And remember, don't cross the line!'

After she had left, I squinted my eyes, but I couldn't see a line anywhere. All I could see was a sea of pink. So much pink, I felt a little ill.

Later that night, while Miranda took her bath, I was alone with Abby. I decided to try and be friendly.

'Nice room you've got,' I squeaked politely.

Abby turned towards me and frowned. 'Were you squeaking at me?' She shook her head. 'This is the last straw. First, I have a room all to myself. Then Mum marries *him* and pretty soon I have a stepsister taking half my room and a new baby brother crying all the time and nobody knows I exist! I'm supposed to be happy about the whole thing when it wasn't my idea. And now they've moved in a guinea pig!'

That wasn't a huge insult, because guinea pigs are cute and furry like me, only not quite as cute. Anyway, I could see Abby's point. I wasn't happy about Og moving into Room 26 and it certainly wasn't my idea! The difference was, Miranda is actually nice. And Og is, well, Og.

Miranda returned and the two girls settled into their respective beds.

'Night, Humphrey,' Miranda said to me.

Neither girl said a word to the other.

I had a long night ahead of me, and since I'm nocturnal and do most of my sleeping during the day, I had a lot of time to think.

What Abby had told me helped me to understand why she was so crabby with Miranda. If only I'd studied psychology like Natalie, maybe I could get inside her head and work out how to make her like Miranda as much as I did.

The next morning, Miranda cleaned my cage while Abby lounged on the bed, writing in her diary.

'What are you doing anyway?' she asked Miranda.

'Taking out the old bedding, putting in new. Changing the water, stuff like that.'

Abby slammed her diary shut. 'It doesn't – you know – go to the toilet in there, does it?'

'Well, of course.'

Abby leaped off her bed and pointed to the door. 'That's the most disgusting thing I've ever heard. Get it out of my room right now!'

(I've worked out a lot about humans, but I still don't know why my little potty corner is always such a big deal to them. I'm really quite tidy.)

Miranda didn't budge. 'He's on my side of the room.'

I was all for Miranda. On the other paw, I could see that Abby had been through a lot of changes in a short time. It's not easy getting a new roommate. I learned that the hard way! I also knew what a good friend Miranda can be. Friends help friends, so I figured it was time I did something about it.

I had a Plan. A Plan using reverse psychology. Since Miranda had no luck in getting Abby to like her, my Plan would make them *not* like each other even more. (If that was possible.)

OK, it didn't make a lot of sense, but when Natalie used reverse psychology, it worked REALLY-REALLY-REALLY well.

I had the chance to set my Plan in motion a short time later when Mr Golden announced that the whole family was going to a museum.

'Do we *all* have to go?' asked Abby.

'Yes, all of us. We're a family, you know,' said her mum.

Abby wrinkled her nose. 'Even the baby?'

'We'll bring the buggy,' said Miranda's dad. 'He'll like it.'

Despite her grumbling, Abby joined the rest of the family and I soon had the whole house to myself. My Plan would take speed, strength, courage and lots of time. It would be well worth it . . . IF it worked.

Once I was sure they were gone, I opened the lock-that-doesn't-lock and hurried over to Abby's bed. I had been studying it all morning and thought that if I grabbed hold, I could climb the bedspread, paw over paw, like a rope. I was huffing and puffing by the time I reached the top, but I made it! Sitting on top of the bedspread was the purple-and-pink-striped pen Abby used to write in her diary. I gave it a big push and it rolled off the bed and on to the floor.

After that, I scrambled over to Abby's dressing table. There, I found her pink bracelet with ABBY spelled out in purple and white beads. I pushed that on to the floor too.

The next part of my mission was fun. I grabbed the edge of the bedspread and slid DOWN-DOWN-DOWN really fast!

I was far from finished. Next I climbed all the

way up Miranda's bedspread to get to her gold ring with the pink stone, which I pushed on to the floor, along with a red loopy thing she sometimes used to pull back her hair. (You don't expect a boy hamster to know what it's called!)

I was halfway to my goal, and the hardest part of my Plan was yet to come.

All morning, I'd had my eye on a big ball of string on the desk. A long piece of the string hung down almost to the floor. I grabbed it and pulled as hard as I could. More and more string unrolled and fell to the floor. I chewed it off and set to work.

Looping the string around the pen and the bracelet, then holding the string in my teeth, I climbed up Miranda's bedspread again. Whew! Mrs Brisbane says exercise is good for you, but that was work! Once I was on the bed, I tugged on the string, pulling up the pen and the bracelet. (Believe me, for a small hamster, those two items are very heavy!) I carefully laid them both on Miranda's pillow where she couldn't miss them.

As tired as I was, there was no time to rest. I slid down to the floor, looped the string around Miranda's ring and the hair holder and pulled them up on to Abby's bed, laying them on her pillow.

(I'm happy to say those two items were not as heavy as the others.)

When the girls came back, Miranda would find

Abby's belongings on her own pillow. Abby would find Miranda's things on her own pillow.

I scurried back to my cosy cage and closed the door behind me. I wanted to be safe when the fireworks began!

> **Little friends may prove to be great friends.**
> Aesop, writer of fables

7 Fright Night

Abby entered first, plopped down on her bed as usual and sighed a big sigh.

'THAT was fun,' she said. 'Especially when the baby threw up in the restaurant.' I don't think she was actually talking to me, but I listened anyway.

A second later, Miranda came in. 'Hi, Humphrey. Did you miss me?' she asked, bending down close to my cage.

'Of course!' I squeaked.

'I suppose you understand what it's saying,' Abby said sourly.

'Sort of,' said Miranda. 'I think he's trying to tell me he missed me.'

Bingo!

I watched Abby closely as she reached for her diary and pen. 'Where's my pen?' she asked. She looked at her pillow. 'What's this stuff doing here?'

Miranda pointed at Abby's bed. 'Hey, that's my hair scrunchie!'

So that's what the hair thing is called!

'And my ring!' Miranda jumped up, crossed over the imaginary line and grabbed her things. 'You took them!'

Abby spotted something on Miranda's pillow. 'There's my pen! You took it! And my name bracelet!' She snatched her items and glared at Miranda. 'You're always taking my things.'

'You took my things! I didn't touch yours,' Miranda insisted. I had never heard her sound that angry before.

Abby's face turned red. 'Why would I take your dinky ring and your stupid scrunchie? I have my own ring and my own scrunchie!'

'Why would I take your stupid pen and a bracelet with your name on it? And why would I put them on my pillow where you can see them?' asked Miranda.

'Just to be mean?'

'I'm not mean!' said Miranda. 'Anyway, isn't it weird that my things were on your pillow and your things were on my pillow?'

Abby thought for a moment. 'Like somebody planned it.'

'Like somebody wanted us to notice,' agreed Miranda.

Suddenly, they were actually talking instead of arguing. I crossed my paws. This had to work!

Abby sat back down on her bed. 'Who would do that? My mum wouldn't. Or your dad.'

Miranda collapsed on to her bed. 'Well, the baby didn't do it.' She started to giggle.

'Maybe Humphrey did it,' said Abby, and she started to giggle.

I chuckled too.

'Those things didn't fly from bed to bed,' said Miranda. 'Somebody put them there on purpose.'

'Or some*thing*,' said Abby. 'Like a . . . a ghost!'

Miranda turned pale. 'You don't have ghosts here, do you?'

'No,' said Abby, shaking her head. 'At least I don't think we do.'

'There are no such things as ghosts,' insisted sensible Miranda. She sounded like she was trying to convince herself.

'NO-NO-NO, there aren't any ghosts, except in stories,' I squeaked. I think I was trying to convince myself.

'I know,' said Abby. She opened her diary and tore out a page. 'I'll write down every possibility of who could have done this. Number one: Miranda.'

'I didn't!' Miranda protested.

'I'm just writing down all the possibilities. Miranda, me, my mum, your dad, Ben, Humphrey. They're the only ones in the house – right? Unless there was a burglar.'

The fur on my back stood straight up. Burglars are scary things!

'Burglars break windows and steal things,' Miranda pointed out. 'The doors were locked, the windows were locked and nothing was stolen.'

'I'm writing all this down. Burglar. Ghost.' Abby quietly stared at the paper for a moment. 'Would you swear you didn't do it?'

'Of course,' said Miranda.

'And I'd swear I didn't do it. Hey, wait a second! Maybe it was Humphrey!' Abby jumped up and walked over to my cage. She bent down and checked the door. 'Nope. It couldn't be him because his door is locked.'

Thank goodness that old lock-that-doesn't-lock fools them every time!

'The only thing on the list that makes sense is a ghost,' she announced.

'But it doesn't make sense,' said Miranda.

'I know,' Abby agreed.

The girls actually agreed on something. This was progress! They'd gone from not liking each other to being REALLY-REALLY-REALLY mad, to talking things over.

After a while, the girls left the room to have supper. This time, they left together. When they came back much later, they were still together.

'Dad said it didn't make sense,' Miranda was saying.

'And Mum agreed,' Abby replied. 'What now?'

The girls flopped down on their respective beds. 'I know,' said Abby. 'Let's stay up all night.'

'Why?'

'To see if any ghosts show up.'

I felt a chill creep down my spine. I knew I was the one who moved their things around. And I knew I wasn't a ghost. But I still got a shiver thinking something SCARY-SCARY-SCARY just might show up.

'Lights out, ladies.' Mr Golden stood at the door later that night, smiling. 'Hope you have sweet dreams. You too, Humphrey.'

'Thanks!' I squeaked back.

'Everybody all tucked in?' Amy appeared at the door, holding baby Ben.

'Yes, Mum.' Abby snuggled down in her bed and pulled up the covers.

'Good night,' said Miranda, pulling up her blanket as well.

The lights went out and it was DARK-DARK-DARK in the room, except for the night-light in the wall, which gave off a pink glow.

The girls were quiet for a few minutes. Then Abby whispered, 'Are you awake?'

'Yes,' Miranda whispered back.

'Know any scary stories?' asked Abby.

I certainly knew a few. Like about the time Clem the dog almost ate me. Or the time Aldo first came into the room at night and I thought he was a ghost.

Miranda thought for a minute and said, 'I remember one from camp.'

'Tell it,' said Abby. 'But not too loud.'

Miranda – sweet Golden Miranda – told a fur-raising tale about a hitchhiker who turned out to be a ghost. The way she told it was scarier than facing Clem!

'That was a good one,' said Abby. 'I know one too.'

Her story was even worse. It was about a group of kids who dared each other to go into a graveyard at night. One girl went in, saw a horrible face and died of fright. Recalling Og's gruesome grin, I felt faint after that story!

'Abby?' Miranda whispered. 'Maybe we shouldn't tell any more scary stories. I'm feeling kind of weird.'

'Me too,' said Abby. 'Let's be quiet.'

It was quiet all right. Maybe a little too quiet for a nocturnal fellow like me. Without thinking, I hopped on to my wheel for some exercise. I suppose that wheel needs oil, because it went *SCREEEECH*!

When the wheel screeched, both girls screamed, 'EEEEEE!' By the little pink light, I could see them leap from their beds and wrap their arms around each other.

The door abruptly swung open and the big light came on.

'EEEEE!' the girls screamed again.

'It's just me,' said Mr Golden, rushing in. 'What's going on?'

He must have been as surprised as I was to see Miranda and Abby hugging one another for dear life.

'There was this terrible noise!' said Abby.

'Horrible,' said Miranda.

That was my cue to hop back on to the wheel. *SCREEEECH*!

All eyes were on me.

'You mean that noise?' said Miranda's dad, pointing at my cage.

'That's the one,' I squeaked.

Both girls started giggling.

'It was Humphrey,' said Miranda.

'I thought it was a ghost,' said Abby.

Mr Golden laughed too. 'I think that ghost is pretty harmless,' he said. 'Now, do you think you two – or you three – can get some sleep?'

They agreed and he tucked the girls into their beds.

'It's good to hear you two laughing, but no more screaming, OK?' he said as he turned out the light.

The girls were quiet for a while longer and I stayed away from the wheel. I heard Abby whisper, 'Miranda, could you sleep over here with me, just for tonight?'

'I was going to ask you the same thing,' said Miranda.

Miranda crawled into bed with Abby.

'Did you ever hear the story about the ghost in the attic?' Abby whispered.

'Tell it,' said Miranda.

And she did. I couldn't have slept that night, even if I wasn't nocturnal.

On Sunday morning, neither girl mentioned how the ring and the bracelet, the pen and the hair scrunchie all got moved. Neither girl mentioned an imaginary line either. They did their homework at the desk, braided each other's hair and made a maze for me to run.

And when they said goodbye on Monday morning, Miranda said, 'See you in two weeks.'

Abby said, 'Great!'

> **All things are in common among friends.**
> Diogenes, Greek philosopher

8 Ill Will

I returned to school with a great sense of accomplishment.

But once I remembered where Og had spent the last two days, it was hard to concentrate on geography or maths. I couldn't help imagining all the fun Og must have had with the Brisbanes. I glanced over at my neighbour in his glass tank. With that horrible grin on his face, he looked like a Hallowe'en lantern. (Scary.)

It was VERY-VERY-VERY cold outside, which meant that the heat inside was turned way, way up. Whew! That must be fine for a cold-blooded amphibian, but I was wishing I could take off my fur coat. Then the warm air woke up the crickets, who started singing. And there was a SQUEAK-SQUEAK-SQUEAK that was not coming from me, but from Seth as he wriggled in his chair. It sounded like 'Jingle Bells': Squeak-squeak-squeak ... squeak-squeak-squeak ... squeak-squeak-SQUEAK-squeak-squeak! The squeaking made Gail giggle noisily, which made Mrs Brisbane loudly shush her. I was looking forward to some peace and quiet during break (knowing Og wouldn't want to chat). But when the time came, Mrs Brisbane announced that the class would stay inside. She brought out all kinds of interesting things to play with. I must admit, I wished I could get out of my cage and play along with the rest of the class.

Art and Richie built a tall tower out of tiny bricks, while Kirk and Seth worked on a jigsaw puzzle. A.J. and Garth played a game where you slapped down cards. Heidi and Gail played another kind of game, moving little plastic men around a board. Mandy, Sayeh and Miranda came over to ask Tabitha to play with them. She didn't even look up. She just shook her head.

'I don't know why we even try to be friends with her,' Mandy whispered to the other girls.

Sayeh just sighed sadly. I knew how she felt.

'Og, can you hear me?' I squeaked. 'I have something to ask you.' I figured even though I couldn't understand him, maybe he could understand me.

'See how much fun it is to play with your friends?'

I asked. It probably sounded like 'Squeak-squeak-squeak,' but he could at least have responded with a 'Boing!'

I decided to squeak up louder this time. I couldn't even hear myself because of all the yelling.

Yelling?

I looked around to see who was making all that noise. It wasn't Lower-Your-Voice-A.J. or Repeat-It-Please-Richie. It was Gail. She had stopped giggling and started shouting. The person she was shouting at was her best friend Heidi.

'You cheated! I saw you!' she yelled.

'I didn't,' Heidi said. 'I wouldn't cheat.'

'You must have. You always win. I'm never playing with you again, cheat,' Gail shouted.

Mrs Brisbane quickly moved towards them. 'Girls, please!'

'I didn't cheat,' insisted Heidi. 'I'm not a cheat.'

Gail put her fingers in her ears. 'Did too, cheat, cheat, cheat!'

Everyone else in the class stopped playing and stared at the two girls. Mrs Brisbane was right between them now. 'Girls, please calm down and be quiet.'

Heidi and Gail were quiet, but they glared at each other angrily.

'Tell me what happened, Gail. Calmly.'

Gail wiped away some tears. 'She was supposed

to move her man five spaces and she moved it six spaces. That gave her a bonus jump and she won. She cheated!'

'Did not!' Heidi shouted. 'I only went five!'

The teacher held up both hands. 'Stop. I want you two to cool off before we talk about it. You're such good friends, let's work this out.'

'She's not my friend any more!' said Gail. She was crying harder.

'Thank goodness!' Heidi shot back. 'Because I can't stand you! Crybaby!'

'Cheat!'

Mrs Brisbane shook her head. 'Heidi, you go over there by Humphrey and Og,' she said firmly. 'Gail, you go and sit at my desk. Try and settle down.'

The girls did as they were told. I think they were glad to get away from each other. Soon, Heidi was leaning up against the table where Og and I have our homes.

'Crybaby,' she whispered so softly that only we could hear her.

It was hard for me to believe that Heidi would cheat her best friend. It was hard for me to believe that Gail would lie about Heidi. I thought friends always got along, no matter what.

'First, all she does is giggle. Now all she does is cry,' Heidi muttered.

At Mrs Brisbane's desk, Gail glared over at Heidi and wiped away a few more tears.

When break was almost over, Mrs Brisbane took the two girls out into the corridor to discuss the argument. They came back in and quietly returned to their seats. But as soon as Mrs Brisbane turned her back, I saw them stick their tongues out at each other. Maybe friendship wasn't all it was cracked up to be.

It was snowing by afternoon break, so Mrs Brisbane divided the class into four teams. Each team had questions to answer. They had to decide as a group what the answer should be. Mrs Brisbane kept score.

She wisely put Heidi and Gail on different teams so they wouldn't argue or make faces. Both their teams lost.

The winning team had Miranda, Kirk, Seth and Tabitha on it. And, to my surprise, the reason they won was Tabitha!

Mrs Brisbane asked each team questions about all kinds of things: flowers, books, poetry, sport, animals (but not hamsters, I'm sorry to say) and countries. Nobody knew much about flowers. Everybody knew a lot about animals. Sayeh was the best at answering questions about countries. (Would you believe, there's a country with a capital called Tegucigalpa? I had to write that one down.)

But Tabitha was the best at answering questions

about sport. She knew soccer teams, volleyball rules and golf champions. The boys all seemed amazed. As the quiz went on, there seemed to be more and more questions about sport. Maybe that was an accident, but when Mrs Brisbane is involved, things don't usually happen by chance.

By the end of break, Tabitha's team had scored forty points. They would have scored even higher if Kirk hadn't said that the Gettysburg Address was the number on the Gettysburg family home. (Even I know it was a speech written by a very famous American president.) He got a laugh and lost two points, but it didn't matter. The next closest team only had twenty-eight points.

'We won!' yelled Seth, the team captain. 'Way to go!' He high-fived Tabitha, Miranda and Kirk.

'Three cheers for Tabitha!' said Miranda.

'Hip hip hooray! Hip hip hooray! Hip hip hooray!' I squeaked, jumping up and down for joy.

Nobody called her a baby. Even Tabitha looked happy.

Unfortunately, Heidi and Gail didn't seem cheered up at all. In fact, while all the attention was focused on Tabitha, I saw Gail mouth 'cheat' to Heidi.

Heidi stuck her tongue out at Gail.

It was enough to make a grown hamster cry. A less sensible hamster than me, of course.

'Og, you may not understand me, but if you could, you'd want Heidi and Gail to be friends again. Right?' I asked my neighbour once everyone had gone home for the day. I didn't expect him to understand me. I was just thinking out loud.

I was amazed to get an answer: 'BOING!'

Og jumped straight up and down, up and down, over and over again. I didn't know if he had sat on a needle or eaten something that didn't agree with him.

'Og! Are you all right?'

'BOING-BOING!' he said. 'BOING!'

I jumped up and looked over at him. I was pretty sure he was agreeing with me!

'So what are we going to do?' I asked him. 'How can we help them?'

As abruptly as he had begun, Og stopped bouncing and boinging and sat as still as a rock, as usual. I was discouraged, and puzzled too. Either he didn't have any ideas or he'd given up on trying to get me to understand him. I felt we both had failed.

Finally, I spoke again. 'They sure were good friends.'

Og stayed silent the rest of the night.

Hours later, when Aldo arrived, I was still trying to work out what google-eyes had been trying to tell me. This was a most peculiar frog.

'Good evening, gentlemen. Mind if I join the party?' said Aldo as he flicked on the lights and rolled his cleaning trolley into Room 26.

'Without you, there is no party,' I told him.

'Speaking of parties, Richie is having a big party for his birthday soon.' Repeat-It-Please-Richie Rinaldi happened to be Aldo's nephew. 'It's going to be a very big deal.'

Since I had never been to one, any birthday party sounded special to me.

'They're having entertainment, like a show or something. Hey, you guys want to see my latest trick?' asked Aldo, grabbing his broom.

The caretaker had already proved his talents to me by balancing his broom on the tip of one finger for a LONG-LONG-LONG time. Once, he balanced it on top of his head.

This time, he threw his head back and balanced the tip of the broom on his chin for an equally long period of time. When the broom finally wobbled too far, Aldo caught it and took a deep bow.

'Bravo, Aldo!' I squeaked as loudly as I could.

'Thank you, Humph.' He glanced at Og. 'What's the matter, Froggy? You don't like tricks?'

'It's not you,' I said softly. 'It's him.'

Aldo grabbed his bag and pulled a chair close to my cage. 'Aw, it's just a silly trick. I'm not good at anything useful.'

'Not true!' I argued.

Aldo took a sandwich out of his bag and began chewing on it.

'No, Humph, I've been thinking about it a lot. Because of this.' He pulled a piece of paper out of his pocket.

'This is the application for City College. If I want to go there, I have to fill it in. So I wrote my name, address, all that. When I got to the part that asked what I want to study, I got stuck,' he explained. 'I'm practically middle-aged and I still don't know what I want to be when I grow up.' Aldo put down his sandwich and stared at the application.

'I'm not sure what I'm good at. I thought of being a teacher, but I don't know. Would the kids like me? Am I clever enough to be a really good teacher?'

'Yes! Be a teacher! Please!' I insisted. For once, Aldo didn't seem to hear me.

'Besides, they want a letter of recommendation from somebody important. Somebody who believes I can succeed,' said Aldo.

'I'll do it!' I assured him, but he wasn't paying attention.

'I'm just not sure.' He tossed his bag back on to

the trolley. 'Don't think I forgot you, pal,' he told me as he dropped a small piece of carrot into my cage.

'Thanks a heap!' I squeaked.

'You're welcome,' Aldo replied.

At least *he* understood most of what I said. One thing I understood: it was time for me to take action!

> **Never injure a friend, even in jest.**
> Cicero, Roman writer and orator

9 Mrs Brisbane Explains

After the caretaker left, I noticed something odd beside my cage. Aldo was usually good at picking up things that didn't belong in the classroom. However, this night he had left something behind: his City College application. I opened the good old lock-that-doesn't-lock and slipped out of my cage.

'Don't worry, Oggy old boy. I won't bother you if you won't bother me,' I assured him. Maybe I was reassuring myself he wouldn't leap at me again.

The application was a big piece of paper that folded up. Half of it was stuck under my cage, and it was hard to read what Aldo had written. If you're a small hamster, human handwriting looks HUGE-HUGE-HUGE. The only light I had to read by was from the streetlamp outside the window. I squinted my eyes and I could read: AREA OF STUDY. On the line next to it, Aldo had written 'Teaching' and scratched it out.

On the line marked RECOMMENDATION, he hadn't written anything.

I was tempted to get out my little pencil and write a nice recommendation myself. But a big college probably wouldn't care about the opinion of a small hamster, even a classroom hamster who could read and write. No, Aldo needed help from someone a lot bigger and more important than me.

I knew who that person was. I just hoped she would help.

I pulled the application out farther and neatly left it right between my cage and Og's.

'No splashing over here, Og,' I warned my neighbour. 'We want to keep this application in good shape.'

He didn't splash all night long. Who knows, maybe Og understood me after all, even without ears.

·ö·

I could hardly wait for Mrs Brisbane to arrive the following morning. When she finally turned up, it took her a long time to take off her coat and gloves and arrange her desk. At last, she strolled – slowly – over to my cage.

'Morning, Humphrey,' she said with a smile.

'You're lucky you don't have to go out in this freezing cold weather. You can stay right here in your cosy cage.'

Stay in my cage? If she only knew!

She turned to Og. 'Morning, Og. As you've heard in class, amphibians are cold-blooded, which means we've got to keep you warm.'

She smiled at Og and turned away.

'Wait! Stop!' I shouted, jumping up and down. 'Look at the paper!'

She turned back and laughed. 'What's the matter, Humphrey? Are you jealous of Og?' She leaned closer. 'You know you're my favourite hamster. And you mustn't let jealousy, that old green-eyed monster, get the better of you.'

Eeek – a monster? I was about to dive into my sleeping house for protection, but then I remembered that jealousy is when you envy somebody else. Jealousy wasn't a real monster, just a giant bad feeling. Was that why I felt bad when everybody else paid attention to Og? I wasn't sure. After all, my eyes are brown, not green. I was trying to sort it all out when Mrs Brisbane turned to walk away.

I'd forgotten something REALLY-REALLY-REALLY important!

'The application!' I shouted. I knew all she'd hear was squeaking, but I had to try.

Mrs Brisbane came back to the cage. 'For goodness' sake, calm down, Humphrey.'

I didn't calm down. I started squeaking and jumping, jumping and squeaking, because I couldn't think of anything else to do ... except open the cage door and hand her the application.

I couldn't do that because she'd find out about the lock-that-doesn't-lock.

'What's this?' Mrs Brisbane picked up the application – phew! – and started to read! 'Aldo must have left this here by mistake. I'll put it in his letterbox.'

She folded it up without finishing it.

'Tell her, Og! Help me ... help Aldo!' I was shrieking more than squeaking now, and to my amazement, Og let out a rather large 'BOING!' which I really appreciated.

'What's the matter with you two? It's an application. It's private.'

'BOING! BOING!'

'SQUEAK-SQUEAK-SQUEAK!'

Working together, we kept up the noise-making and Mrs Brisbane looked confused. She opened the application and started reading – thank goodness, because I was getting quite hoarse.

'Well, well. Aldo is applying to go back to college. That's a good idea. And he wants to study ...' She stopped and stared a bit longer. 'He wrote in "Teaching" but crossed it out again. I wonder why?'

'Ask him!' I shouted with the last bit of my voice.

'I'd better give Aldo a ring,' said Mrs Brisbane.

'Hi, Mrs Brisbane!' a loud voice yelled. It was Lower-Your-Voice-A.J.

Mrs Brisbane greeted him and folded up the application. She took it to her desk and didn't look at it again all day.

There was nothing to do now but keep my paws firmly crossed, which I did.

·ö·

Some time in the afternoon, I must have dozed off, but I was awakened by a now familiar noise: 'Chirrup!' That was the sound of a cricket. This time, it was coming from the middle of the room.

'Mrs Brisbane?' a voice called out.

'Chirrup!'

Our teacher turned away from the board, where she was writing out a maths problem. 'Yes, Kirk?'

'I think a cricket has got loose.' Kirk pointed to the floor near his table.

'Well, pick it up, please,' Mrs Brisbane said.

'Chirrup! Chirrup!'

Kirk bent down and cupped his hands, touching the floor. 'I've got it!'

'Good. Now please put it back where it belongs.'

Kirk lifted his hands and sat upright in his chair. 'I don't know, Mrs Brisbane. I think it might get away.'

Everyone was watching as Kirk stood up and started walking towards the cabinet where the crickets were kept. As he passed by Heidi, he suddenly opened his hands up right over her head. 'Oops! Dropped it. Sorry, Heidi.'

Heidi leaped up and started jumping around the room, shaking her head and running her hands through her hair. 'Help! Get it off me. Get it off!' she screamed.

Everyone was laughing. Everyone except Mrs Brisbane.

'Kirk Chen, you find that cricket,' she said in a very stern tone of voice. 'Now!'

Kirk grinned. 'Aw, there was no cricket. I was making that noise.'

Heidi stopped jumping around and glared at him.

'Hear it? Chirrup. Chirrup.' Kirk really sounded like a cricket. 'Boy, that Heidi Hopper sure can hop!' he added.

Gail giggled until Heidi shot her a very angry look, then quickly covered her mouth to stop herself.

Mrs Brisbane slowly walked towards Kirk. 'You, my friend, are in trouble. Big trouble,' she said.

'You will stay in during break and we'll have a little talk.'

As Kirk returned to his seat, the room was very quiet. Except for a loud 'Chirrup!'

Without even turning to look at him, Mrs Brisbane said, 'I-Heard-That-Kirk Chen.'

I wouldn't have wanted to be Kirk when it was time for break. Once the other students had cleared out, Mrs Brisbane marched over to him. Boy, was he in trouble! So I was surprised at the first thing she said.

'I have a confession to make. I think you're a funny guy, Kirk. You make me laugh a lot. Some day, you might star in a funny movie, and I promise you, I'll be the first one in the queue to buy a ticket.'

Kirk looked as confused as I felt.

'But –' Uh-oh, here came the clincher. 'There's a time to be funny and a way to be funny that's appropriate. And there's a time to be funny and a way to be funny that is not. It's time for you to learn the difference.'

I waited for a 'Chirrup', or at least an argument, but Kirk remained silent.

'Why did you pretend to drop a cricket on Heidi's head?' Mrs Brisbane asked.

Kirk shrugged his shoulders. 'Because it was funny?'

'Do you think Heidi thought it was funny?'

Kirk shook his head.

'I think you did it to get attention. And if that's the case, it worked.' I'm not sure, but I think Mrs Brisbane smiled. 'Now, why do you like to get attention?'

Kirk shrugged again.

'So people will like you?' the teacher asked.

'Maybe.'

'Then I have good news for you. You don't have to play pranks any more. People already like you. You're one of the most popular students I have.'

I'm not sure, but I think Kirk smiled a little too.

'So the next time you think of doing something funny, I want you to think about two things. First: is it really funny? Or is it hurtful to someone? Second: are you just doing it to get attention? Can you work on that?'

'Yes, ma'am,' said Kirk.

'Because if you continue to act like you acted today, I'm afraid you're going to be doing a solo comedy act in the headmaster's office. And he may not think you're funny at all.'

I think Mr Morales has a good sense of humour. But I also think that Mrs Brisbane is good at working out what's going on in people's heads. I bet she studied psychology in college.

Kirk was quiet for the rest of the day. So were Og and the crickets.

∙ö∙

After my classmates went home, Mrs Brisbane hung around longer than usual. I soon learned why. Aldo came to Room 26 to see her.

'Mrs Brisbane, thanks for your call,' he said.

'And I thank you for coming in early to talk,' she said.

They looked funny sitting in those little student chairs.

'I hope you'll forgive me for reading this application you left behind. It was none of my business,' she explained.

Maybe not, but I'd made sure it was her business, with a little help from Og.

'When I saw that you had written in "Teaching" and then crossed it out, I thought perhaps you'd like to talk.'

'Yes, I would,' said Aldo. He was strangely quiet, and I suppose he was nervous, because he kept tugging at his collar. 'I was thinking I'd like to be a teacher, but I'm kind of . . . afraid.'

Mrs Brisbane listened while Aldo explained his fears about not being clever enough or interesting enough to be a good teacher.

'Everybody feels that way,' she said with a warm

smile. 'What makes you think you would like to teach?'

Was I surprised to hear Aldo talk about how much he liked books, science, history, maths, learning . . . how much he liked children! (He didn't mention hamsters, but I knew how he felt about me.)

When he had finished, Mrs Brisbane laughed out loud. 'You'd better become a teacher or I'll be angry with you. You sound like a born teacher!'

'How can I know for sure?' Aldo asked.

'Would you like to try it out?' Mrs Brisbane asked.

'Try out . . . teaching?'

'Yes. We'll pick a day for you to come in and teach a subject to the class. You can choose any subject. See how it feels to be in front of a classroom. See how the students react to you.'

Aldo rose and began to pace up and down. 'That's a wonderful offer. I don't know. Sounds good. Maybe.'

'Please think about it, talk it over with your wife and let me know,' Mrs Brisbane suggested. 'But you'll have to do it soon. This application is due in a week.'

'I will, I will,' said Aldo. 'If I could be half the teacher you are, I'd be happy.'

Mrs Brisbane laughed. 'Thank you, Aldo. But even after all these years, I still have my bad days.'

Aldo shook her hand about ten times before leaving.

Mrs Brisbane gathered together her things, and when she was ready to leave for the day, she turned to Og and me. 'Hope you're satisfied, guys,' she said.

I don't know about Og, but believe me, I was HAPPY-HAPPY-HAPPY.

·ö·

I wasn't surprised that Mrs Brisbane helped Aldo. It happened just the way I planned it. But the next day, I had a big surprise I never could have planned.

My classmates were all hurrying out of Room 26, heading for the canteen. Usually, Sit-Still-Seth would have raced out of the room. But on this day, he hung behind the others.

'Coming?' Kirk asked impatiently.

'Meet you there,' said Seth.

Seth was the only student left in the room except for Tabitha, who was trying to stuff Smiley into her pocket as Seth approached.

I couldn't imagine what he was doing. Tabitha had given the girls the cold shoulder when they tried to be friends. And Seth is a boy. Everybody knows boys and girls can't be friends. At least, that's what I heard Art and Richie say.

'How'd you know all that sport stuff the other day?' he asked her.

Tabitha shrugged her shoulders. 'I don't know. I just like sport. And I remember things I hear about sport.'

'Me too,' answered Seth. 'What sports do you like best?'

Tabitha thought about it. 'Basketball and baseball. Football. Tennis.'

'Me too,' Seth agreed.

Mrs Brisbane was in the doorway. 'Are you two coming?'

'Right away,' said Seth. But he turned back to Tabitha. 'Listen, I've got to ask. Why do you keep that stupid bear with you? Aren't you too old for that?' he asked.

Tabitha shrugged again.

'When I was little, back in first year, I had a truck I used to bring to school with me. I couldn't stand to be without it,' Seth told her.

'Do you still have it?' asked Tabitha.

'It's in my wardrobe. Sometimes I take it out, but I don't bring it to school any more.'

Mrs Brisbane waited at the door. Now she didn't seem to be in such a hurry to get to lunch.

'My mum gave me Smiley,' Tabitha explained. 'My real mum. I haven't seen her for four years.'

'Oh,' said Seth. 'I get it.'

'You two are going to miss lunch,' Mrs Brisbane reminded them.

'OK.' Seth rushed out of the door, but Tabitha stayed in her seat. Mrs Brisbane came towards her.

'Tabitha, I know you've been moved around a lot. Your foster mother told me you've been with five families in four years. But she also told me that she wants you to stay with her for ever.'

Tabitha stroked Smiley's fur. 'They all say that. It just never works out.'

Mrs Brisbane sat in the chair next to Tabitha so they were eye to eye. 'I don't mind having Smiley in class. But I think you'd make more friends if you left him at home. He'd be waiting for you there. You can make new friends without giving up the old ones. Don't you know that little song?'

Now Mrs Brisbane has surprised me many times, but I almost fell off my ladder when she started to sing.

Make new friends, but keep the old.
One is silver and the other's gold.

What a beautiful song! And Mrs Brisbane had a nice voice too. We were all quiet afterwards until Tabitha asked, 'What's the good of making friends if you're not going to stay?'

'A person can have many friends in her life. Even

if you move on, a friend can be for ever. At least in your memory.'

Oooh, I felt a little pang somewhere close to my heart. Ms Mac was the teacher who brought me to Room 26. Although she had to move on without me, she was a for ever friend who would always be in my memory. Ms Mac was pure gold.

'Listen to her! She's right!' I squeaked.

Mrs Brisbane smiled. 'Sounds like Humphrey wants to be your friend too. How would you like to take him home with you this weekend?'

'I'd have to ask my mum. My foster mum.'

'I'll ring her right now, while you get some lunch,' said the teacher.

I have to admit, Mrs Brisbane is the BEST-BEST-BEST teacher in the world and also a golden friend. Even if she did let Og into the classroom and made us study frogs.

> To like and dislike the same things,
> that is indeed true friendship.
> Sallust, Roman politician
> and historian

10 Test Distress

As Aldo swept the floor later that night, he talked and talked.

'Maria thinks I should take Mrs Brisbane up on her offer. I don't know, Humph. Can you imagine me as a teacher?'

'YES-YES-YES!' I squeaked.

'I mean, what could I teach those kids? What do I know?'

Aldo spent many an evening talking to me while we ate our suppers. Believe me, he knew a lot! But I'd never seen him act like this before. He muttered while he mopped the floor. He mumbled while he dusted. He argued with himself while he sat down to eat his sandwich.

'Science? Maths? History? Which would be best?' he asked.

'Anything except frogs,' I squeaked, and to my surprise, Og responded with a 'Boing!'

'I bet they've learned a lot from you, Humphrey. You've probably taught these kids more than I ever could.'

I was too modest to answer 'Yes.'

Aldo dug down into his bag and pulled out a piece of broccoli. 'Here's something for you, buddy.' He held it up and examined it. 'Funny, it looks small to me, but to you, I bet it looks like a great big tree!'

What it looked like was delicious. 'Thanks,' I squeaked.

Aldo leaned in closer and stared at me. 'I guess everything looks different to you, pal.' He held up his finger. 'I just see a finger, but I'll bet you see every little line and swirl in the skin.'

I wasn't quite sure what Aldo was getting at, but I squeaked in support.

Aldo took a long sip of coffee from his thermos. 'Of course, no two people see things exactly the same, either. And the more you look, the more . . .'

He suddenly jumped up. 'This might be it, Humphrey. I mean, it's interesting, it's different. Like a microscope. Yeah!'

I had no idea what he was talking about, so I munched thoughtfully on the broccoli. (Why some humans don't like it is a mystery to me.)

Aldo wheeled out his cleaning trolley. 'You always give me the best ideas, Humph! See you later!'

He disappeared, but then quickly popped his head back into the doorway.

'You too, Og. Don't want to leave out my fine froggy friend!'

So, Og was Aldo's friend ... but still not mine.

I suppose the grumpy lump next door didn't know or care, because all I heard from him was splashing.

·ö·

Tabitha's foster mum said yes. I'd be spending the weekend at her house. But I figured I wouldn't get much attention from Tabitha since all she cared about was Smiley the bear.

There were SO many problems in Room 26. Garth and A.J. were still worried about Marty Bean. Heidi and Gail were still MAD-MAD-MAD. Miranda and Abby were friends now, but would they stay that way without me around to help? I spent so much time thinking about these problems, I forgot the other problems in Room 26.

Maths problems.

I had been dreaming (the sleeping kind and the day kind) during maths for most of the week. When Mrs Brisbane started revising for a big maths test coming up, I had no idea what she was talking about!

I wasn't alone. Mrs Brisbane gave the class a surprise quiz and guess what? Half of us failed!

'It's not fair!' Mandy complained, while everybody else moaned and groaned. Our teacher was not pleased.

'All right, class. The quiz won't count towards your marks. But the rest of the school year builds on these concepts. You've got to master these problems,' she explained. 'I've prepared a study guide for the test next week. I want you to complete this over the weekend.'

You should have heard the moans and groans then!

'I'm sorry, class. This is important to me and to you,' Mrs Brisbane insisted as she handed out the papers. 'Put your name on your guide and bring it back – completed – on Monday.'

'I flunked. How about you?' Seth whispered to Tabitha.

'Almost,' she whispered back.

'It's time for break,' Mrs Brisbane said. 'Put your study guides in your backpacks now so you won't forget them.'

Papers rustled as my classmates tucked away their study guides.

The second hand on the big clock circled around.

TICK-TICK-TICK. Those study guides made me think up a Plan, but I wasn't sure I'd have the time to pull it off.

Once the bell rang, the students rushed to get their coats and raced out of the door. Mrs Brisbane gathered up some papers from her desk and hurried out of the door too. Sometimes she spent break in the staffroom. Luckily, this was one of those days.

There was no time to waste, so I flung open my cage door. 'Og, don't you tell a soul what I'm about to do!' I told my neighbour.

It's not easy to get from my cage to the classroom floor, but I'd mastered a technique. First, I slid down the smooth table leg. It wasn't difficult, but it was a bit too fast for comfort. The way back was more challenging. I couldn't slide back up the leg, so I'd grab on to the cord from the blinds and swing myself back up. It was a dangerous undertaking that was always scary. But I had to take the chance because I had important work to do.

Once I hit the ground, I scampered over to Seth's chair. His backpack was on the floor. Happily, he'd left his study guide sticking out of the pocket. I had to use my paws and teeth to pull it out and drag it over to Tabitha's table.

Getting the paper into the pocket of her backpack – which was my goal – was a challenge. Her backpack was hanging from her chair. The

pocket I wanted was at least a foot off the ground –
awfully high for a small hamster.

By chance, there was a long cord dangling down
from the pocket zipper. Holding the paper firmly in
my teeth, I grabbed on and tried to pull myself up
with all my might.

'BOING!' Og was trying to tell me something,
but what?

Just then, the bell rang. It seemed much louder
than usual. So that's what he was trying to tell me!
He was trying to warn me that I was in serious
danger of being caught outside my cage. I was also
in danger of being trampled on by large feet. At
least they were large compared with me!

I dropped the study guide and scurried as fast as
I could towards the table. With no time to waste,
I grabbed the cord and began swinging back and
forth, higher and higher.

'BOING-BOING!' croaked Og.

'I know, I know!' I squeaked back. My stomach
did flipflops as I saw the edge of the table. I took a
deep breath and leaped on to the tabletop.

Mrs Brisbane opened the door and I could hear the
thunder of feet as my friends rushed to the cloakroom.
I sprinted across the table. Please don't let them see
me. PLEASE-PLEASE-PLEASE, I thought as I
darted into my cage, pulled the door behind me and
collapsed on to a pile of wood shavings.

I held my breath, waiting to hear if I'd been caught in the act. I heard Mrs Brisbane's footsteps approach.

'Why is the cord swinging like that?' she wondered out loud. 'That's odd.'

Og began splashing like I'd never heard him splash before. 'BOING!' he croaked. 'BOING!'

'Calm down, Og,' said Mrs Brisbane. 'Are you hungry or something?' She told Art to feed him some of his beloved insects.

Og had made Mrs Brisbane switch her attention to him, so that she'd forget about the cord. For the first time, I was pretty sure that the frog was talking to me – even helping me. Maybe he was friendlier than I'd thought. He'd helped me get back safely, thank goodness, although my mission had failed.

Once my heartbeat had returned to normal, I squeaked a big 'Thanks' to Og and looked over at Tabitha's table. Seth's study guide was still lying on the floor near her backpack.

Mrs Brisbane talked about something called 'helping verbs' for the rest of the afternoon. When it was almost time for the bell to ring, Mrs Brisbane reminded the class about their maths study guides.

'Tabitha, I believe yours is on the floor. Put it in your backpack, please.'

'Yes!' I squeaked out loud. This was too good to

be true! The bell rang. Seth grabbed his backpack and headed to the cloakroom.

Tabitha didn't bother to look at the paper. She just stuffed it into her backpack pocket. Hooray! She also put Smiley into her bag as the other students streamed out of the classroom.

Soon, Tabitha's mum – her foster mum – arrived to pick us up for the weekend.

When I glanced over at Og, he looked a little gloomy, despite that stupid grin plastered on his face. Maybe he wished he could go home with our classmates at the weekends too. Maybe Og was jealous of me. I had a bad feeling just thinking about that old green-eyed monster again.

Suddenly I felt SAD-SAD-SAD about leaving Og alone for the whole weekend.

A friend is what the heart needs all the time.
Henry Van Dyke, American clergyman, educator and writer

11 Study Buddies

Tabitha's mum looked like the usual kind of mum, even though Tabitha said she wasn't her real one. Tabitha called her Carol.

'I've been looking forward to this all day,' said Carol, with a smile that showed she meant it. I liked her enthusiasm. 'You'll have to show me how to take care of Humphrey. I've never had a hamster before.'

'It's a doddle!' I squeaked.

'I think Humphrey's trying to tell us something,' Carol said. Smart lady!

Once we were home, Carol put my cage on the table and made some hot chocolate. 'How was your day?' she asked.

Tabitha shrugged her shoulders. 'Just like any other day.'

If she only knew!

She opened her backpack and pulled out some papers. 'I've got maths homework.'

Carol examined the paper. 'Honey, this isn't yours. It belongs to somebody named Seth Stevenson.'

Tabitha grabbed the study guide. 'We must have switched.' She rummaged around in her backpack and pulled out another study guide. 'Hang on. This one's mine.' She showed Carol the study guide with her name on it.

'Is this important?' asked Carol.

'Very,' said Tabitha.

'VERY-VERY-VERY.' I couldn't help squeaking up.

'Seth will need this. We'd better try to ring him,' Carol said.

It looked as if things were working out according to my Plan, but you can never be sure with humans.

🐾

Seth and his mum arrived the next morning.

'Thank you for ringing,' said Mrs Stevenson. 'Seth was in a panic when he couldn't find his homework.'

'It took me a while to get your number. I finally called Mrs Brisbane,' Carol explained.

'I'm sorry we never met before. I didn't even know there was a new girl in the class,' Seth's mum said.

Seth and his mother – whose name is June, I

found out – took off their coats, and Carol made hot chocolate again.

'I'm so happy to meet somebody from Tabitha's class,' said Carol.

'Did Tabitha get invited to Richie's birthday party?' June asked.

Carol shook her head.

'I'll ring his mum. She invited everyone in the class, but I'll bet she didn't know about Tabitha either. I'm sorry no one called to welcome you. We'd love to have you at the parent-teacher meetings.'

Carol poured out the steaming chocolate. 'I'd like that. I'm kind of new to the mother business.'

'Looks like you're off to a good start,' said June. The two mothers moved into the living room, while Seth and Tabitha sat by my cage. Smiley the bear lay on the table.

'Hey, Humphrey,' Seth greeted me.

I spun on my wheel to show him I was happy to see him.

'If Richie invites you to his party, will you go?' he asked Tabitha.

'I don't know,' she said. 'Maybe.'

Seth rubbed his nose. 'Well, if you do, could you leave Smiley at home?'

Tabitha looked surprised. 'Why?'

Seth sighed. 'Well, I know you're not weird, but the other kids think you are because of the bear. If you'd leave him at home, they'd know you're – you know – normal, like them. Then they'd like you.'

Tabitha thought it over. 'Are you going to be there?'

'Sure. Richie says he's planned a cool surprise!'

Tabitha frowned. 'I don't like surprises.'

'This will be a good surprise. A great surprise,' said Seth.

Tabitha didn't answer right away. 'OK. If you'll be there, I'll come. And I'll leave Smiley at home.'

Seth looked relieved. 'Great.'

They watched me spin on my wheel and talked about the maths test. After a while, Tabitha said, 'The basketball game's on. Want to watch it?'

The two of them raced out of the room and I didn't see them again for the rest of the afternoon. June went home, but Seth stayed and she picked him up later. I didn't care because I wasn't worried any more.

Tabitha left Smiley on the table next to my cage. He seemed to be smiling even more than usual.

It looked as if a nice, shiny, silver friendship had begun.

·ö·

I felt warm inside all weekend, especially when Seth rang Tabitha on Sunday night to ask her some questions about maths.

But it was COLD-COLD-COLD on Monday. Shivering, quivering cold.

It was even chillier if you were standing near Heidi and Gail. Even when she wasn't around Heidi, Gail hardly ever giggled any more.

Then came Tuesday, the day of the big maths test. It was probably the quietest day of the year, as my classmates were very serious about this test. Kirk groaned a few times during the test. Seth got up three times to sharpen his pencil. Everyone seemed glad when it was over. Especially me.

Aldo was unusually quiet that night too. Instead of talking to me while he ate, he spent a lot of time writing in a big notebook. Sometimes he'd stop to stare at me, then go back to writing.

It started to snow on Thursday. When the students got to class, they were all bundled up in heavy hats and scarves and they all had red noses. (A few of those noses were runny, I'm sorry to say.)

After class began, Mrs Brisbane rubbed her hands together as if they were still cold. 'I have finished marking your maths tests,' she announced. 'Every single mark went up. Most of them a lot. I know how hard you all worked and I'm proud of you. Now we can get back to preparing for the Poetry Festival.'

When she handed the tests back, there were sighs of relief this time and not one groan.

'Now I have a big surprise for you. Today we're going to have a guest teacher.'

'Is that like a supply teacher?' asked Heidi. Of

course, Mrs Brisbane reminded her to raise her hand.

'No. He's coming in to teach one class. And many of you already know him. It's Aldo Amato.'

'You mean my uncle Aldo?' asked Richie.

'Yes, your uncle – Mr Amato,' said Mrs Brisbane.

And there he was at the door. Aldo had become Mr Amato. He wore a white shirt, a red waistcoat, dark trousers and a tartan tie. He looked almost as spiffy as Headmaster Morales, and his cleaning trolley was nowhere in sight.

'Come on in,' Mrs Brisbane said.

'Thank you, Mrs Misbane ... Mrs Bisbrain ... Mrs Brisbane,' Aldo stammered. It might have been cold outside, but Aldo was sweating. I was pretty nervous myself.

He turned to the students and said, 'Hello everybody. I spend a lot of time in this classroom when you're not here, so it's nice to see real people sitting in these chairs for once. A good-looking group, I must say.'

A few students chuckled, and Aldo relaxed a little.

'I was talking to my pal Humphrey the other night and I started thinking about what the world looks like from his point of view. I mean, here he is, a small animal in a room full of much larger animals. Namely – you!'

When everybody laughed, Aldo looked a lot more relaxed.

'Anyway, Humphrey gave me a great idea for something we can all try together today.'

Who, me? Gosh!

Aldo held up a pencil. 'Can anybody tell me what this is?'

'A pencil!' answered Heidi.

'Oops. Hands, please,' said Aldo.

Heidi's hand shot up.

'Yes, ma'am', said Aldo.

I was impressed. Mrs Brisbane never called anybody 'ma'am'.

'It's a pencil,' said Heidi.

'Really? What do you think?' Aldo pointed at Pay-Attention-Art, who was staring up at the ceiling.

'Who, me? What?'

Aldo walked towards Art, holding the pencil up. 'I ask you, sir, what does this look like?'

Mrs Brisbane never called anybody 'sir' either.

'A pencil?' answered Art.

Aldo stared at the pencil for a second. 'I think you're right. But what does it look like to Humphrey?' Aldo asked.

To tell you the truth, I thought it looked like a pencil, but that clearly wasn't the answer Aldo wanted.

He approached my cage and held the pencil up

right in front of me, very close. 'What do you think Humphrey sees?'

The class was quiet for a few seconds before hands began going up. Even Heidi remembered to raise her hand.

Aldo picked Kirk this time.

'He probably sees a big strip of yellow,' he said.

'I think you're right. What do you think?' Aldo pointed to Sayeh.

'Maybe something grainy. Like a yellow tree trunk,' she answered.

'Yeah. If you look closely, you can see the texture.' Aldo turned to me. 'Right, Humph?'

'Whatever you say, Aldo,' I squeaked.

That sent Gail giggling until she caught Heidi's eye. Heidi made a face at her and Gail turned serious.

'So today we're going to look at the world from a Humphrey's-eye point of view. Ready to start?'

My classmates all smiled and nodded. Aldo opened a briefcase – I'd never seen that before – and took out an envelope full of tiny squares that were open in the middle, like picture frames.

'These little squares will help us look at things more closely.'

Aldo must have spent a lot of time cutting out those one-inch squares. He handed one to each student. Next, he took out all kinds of things from his briefcase and spread them on Mrs Brisbane's desk. Coloured leaves, pieces of lettuce, tomato and broccoli, lemon peel, onion skin, heavy paper, a purple feather, pieces of bread – many interesting and yummy things!

'I want you to draw what you see with your coloured pencils or crayons and answer a few questions,' said Aldo. 'OK, you can start exploring now.'

Soon my friends were wandering around the room, examining things through their square inch. They were so BUSY-BUSY-BUSY, no one seemed to notice that Mr Morales had slipped into the room. He and Mrs Brisbane both watched Aldo. They were nodding and smiling.

The kids were smiling too.

'Ooh, you should see this!' A.J. yelled as he viewed his glove through the square.

I was the only one who noticed that Sayeh went over to Tabitha and asked her if she could borrow Smiley and study his fur.

'He's not here,' Tabitha answered. 'He's at home.'

You could have knocked me over with a purple feather!

While my friends looked at the world from a different point of view, I looked at Og. How did he see the world? His goofy eyes pointed in two different directions. Perhaps I looked like two hamsters. Or a much bigger hamster than I am. Maybe that's why he leaped at me the first night. It would take more than looking through a little square for me to figure out Og.

After a while, Aldo asked the kids to return to their seats.

'What did you see?' he asked them.

They couldn't wait to share their discoveries. A.J. said his gloves had a million little squares where the lines of yarn crisscrossed. Art's green leaf had a lot of yellow in it and although it seemed smooth, when you saw it up close it was covered with wrinkles. Og's green skin had black dots in it. According to Mandy, my beautiful golden fur was actually brown and white as well as yellow!

'And what did you learn?' asked Aldo.

Gail raised her hand. 'That things look different when you look at them more closely.'

Aldo smiled broadly. 'Good! You learned to observe.' He wrote the word on the board. 'And observation is what scientists do. Sometimes they use microscopes or telescopes to get a closer look. The more you observe, the more you learn. Today, you took a first step towards being a scientist.'

Wow, I never knew I was in a classroom full of scientists!

The bell rang for break. As they hurried to get their coats, my classmates thanked Aldo one by one. Finally no one was left except Aldo, Mrs Brisbane and Mr Morales the headmaster.

'Excellent job,' said Mrs Brisbane. 'I wish you'd come back and get them excited over maths.'

'Now are you going to send in that application?' asked the headmaster.

Aldo nodded. 'I'm going to do it.'

'I'd like to add something to that application. A letter of recommendation,' said Mrs Brisbane.

I thought Aldo would faint. 'Would you?'

'I'd be proud to write one too,' said Mr Morales.

'I can't thank you enough,' said Aldo.

'Do me one favour,' added the headmaster. 'When you graduate and are ready to start teaching, you come to Longfellow School first.'

Aldo shook his hand. 'I wouldn't go anywhere else,' he said.

Whew! That was a relief. I was SAD-SAD-SAD when Ms Mac left for Brazil. I'd be even sadder if Aldo left too.

> **Tell me your friends and I'll tell you who you are.**
> Assyrian proverb

12 Party Hearty

That week, there was plenty of chatter about Richie's forthcoming birthday. All that excitement gave me a wiggle in my whiskers and a pounding in my heart. What was this big surprise Richie talked about all the time?

On Friday, Mrs Brisbane announced that Richie would be taking me home for the weekend.

'Yeah! Humphrey's coming to the party too,' A.J. yelled.

I'd never been to a party outside Room 26 before. Overjoyed, I jumped on my wheel and spun as fast as I could.

'BOING!' Og croaked.

Oops! I realized that Og had not been invited to the party.

'What about Og?' asked Richie. 'Can he come too?'

Mrs Brisbane shook her head. 'I think you have all you can handle. Besides, I'm taking Og home with me. My husband is working on a surprise for him.'

'Eeek!' I squeaked. It just slipped out. Mr Brisbane, whom I hadn't even seen since Christmas, was working on a surprise for the frog? I could feel that green-eyed monster inside me again. I was jealous of a large lump with a ghastly grin and I wasn't proud of myself.

Richie was hopping from one foot to another, like a frog, by the time his mum came to pick us up after school. 'We're going to party hearty, Humphrey!' he shouted.

'Try to relax, Richie,' Mrs Rinaldi told him as we got into the car. 'If we're going to have this party, you'll have to calm down.'

The Rinaldi house was in quite an uproar that night. First of all, there were so many aunts, uncles, grandmas and grandpas there, I wasn't sure which was which.

Everyone was hustling around, moving chairs and putting up decorations in the basement, or bustling around the kitchen, cooking. As busy as they were, they all managed to stop and say, 'Hi, Humphrey.' Or, 'Isn't he a cutie?'

Uncle Aldo and his wife Maria came round to help. When Aldo announced he was starting college again, his relatives slapped him on the back and said, 'Way to go!' They were as HAPPY-HAPPY-HAPPY about it as I was!

·ö·

On Saturday morning, there was even more commotion as Richie's family hurried up and down the stairs, preparing for the party. Aldo and Maria came back to help. Early in the afternoon, Aldo put on a top hat and picked up my cage.

'OK, Humph. Time for us to party on!'

He carried my cage downstairs to the basement.

What sights I saw there! The ceiling was covered with balloons of every colour. Along the walls were brightly coloured booths made out of big cardboard boxes. A circle of chairs surrounded a large platform. Happy circus music was playing and I could smell popcorn and lemonade.

Aldo put my cage on a big table and said, 'Welcome to Richie Rinaldi's Crazy Carnival! Step right up, one and all!'

Soon my friends from Room 26 made their way down the stairs. Gail and Heidi (not together, of course), Kirk, Garth, Mandy, Sayeh, A.J. and Art, Miranda, Seth and Tabitha.

As soon as Sayeh saw Tabitha arrive, she

hurried over to greet her. 'Oh, I'm glad you came!' she said.

Then, down the stairs came Marty. Marty? I blinked hard and looked again. Sure enough, Martin Bean, the guy who's REALLY MEAN, was right there in Richie's basement!

'My mum made me invite him,' I heard Richie tell Garth. 'He's in my Sunday-school class.'

There's school on Sunday too? You learn something new every day.

The kids all put brightly wrapped presents on a table. Most of them said hello to me. Then Aldo said, 'Step right up and play the most amazing games on earth!'

Each of the booths along the wall featured a different activity. Richie's dad had a booth where the kids tossed rings at empty lemonade bottles. If three rings landed over the bottles, you got a pink ticket.

Cousin Mark's booth featured a game where you threw a small basketball through a hoop. You got a pink ticket for each basket made.

In Grandpa Rinaldi's booth, you had to knock little bowling pins down with a ball. If you knocked them all down, you got a pink ticket.

Closest to me was Maria's booth. She had a flowered scarf on her head and a big glass ball in front of her. 'Come and hear Madame Maria tell your fortune,' she called to the crowd.

Madame Maria told Mandy that, in the future, she would eat 'much popcorn'. (I think she already had.) Then Maria told Kirk that, in the future, he would have a lot of fun. Kirk always does!

There was so much noise in Richie's basement, I was tempted to go into my sleeping house for some peace and quiet. But I didn't want to miss any of the fun.

Then – uh-oh – I noticed someone not having fun. Heidi Hopper was on her way to the basketball booth when Big Mean Bean stood in front of her, blocking her way. She moved to the right to go around him. Marty moved to the right and blocked her.

'What's your hurry?' he asked in a nasty voice.

Heidi moved to the left to go around him. Marty moved to the left and blocked her.

'Say the magic word,' said Marty.

'Please,' Heidi said in a soft voice.

'Can't hear you!'

'Please!' Heidi spoke much louder now.

Marty sneered. 'That's not the magic word. Guess again.'

Once more, Heidi tried to go around him and he stopped her. She was almost in tears. This was unsqueakable behaviour!

'Let her go!' I yelled. Not that anyone could hear a small hamster over all the hubbub.

Suddenly Gail appeared out of nowhere. 'Stop it, Marty!' she said, and she pushed him out of the way. She grabbed Heidi's hand and pulled her towards the fortune-telling booth. 'Come on, Heidi.'

Marty stood there with his mouth wide open. I could hardly believe what I'd seen myself. First of all, I thought Gail was angry at Heidi. Second of all, no younger kid had ever dared to push Marty before. Especially not a girl. Gail's a lot stronger than she looks.

'Yoohoo, ladies! Fortunes told! Let Madame Maria tell you what your future will bring!'

Heidi and Gail looked at one another.

'Step this way,' Maria called to them.

The two girls scurried over to her booth and sat down as Maria stared into the glass ball.

'You will be best friends for ever,' Maria predicted. Hooray! Heidi and Gail looked happy with their fortunes. As they walked away, I heard Gail say, 'I'm sorry I said you were a cheat. I was wrong.'

'I'm sorry I called you a crybaby,' said Heidi.

They didn't seem to know what else to say, until Mandy raced up and asked if they'd tried the ring-toss yet. The three of them hurried off to the booth. Those old, gold friends, Heidi and Gail, were back together at last.

Meanwhile, Marty seemed puzzled by the whole incident. He stood motionless, watching the other partygoers pairing off and having fun together. I guess Aldo was watching, because he marched over to him and said, 'If you need something to do, I could use some help giving out prizes.'

Marty didn't answer.

'Or would you rather be with your friends? You do have friends, don't you, Marty?'

Marty stood like a statue, staring at Aldo.

'You know, Marty, if you stopped pushing everybody around, people might start liking you. So why don't you come over and do something nice, like handing out prizes?'

Aldo didn't wait for an answer. He put his hand on Marty's shoulder and marched him to the prize booth.

Meanwhile, Richie and Seth cheered on Tabitha as she got three baskets in a row. Smiley the bear was nowhere in sight.

After Miranda and Sayeh had each earned a handful of pink tickets, they headed for the prize booth. But when they saw Marty there, they stopped in their tracks.

'I'm not going over there if he's there,' said Miranda. 'He'd probably steal my tickets.'

A.J. and Art were already at the prize booth, trying to choose from the assortment of little puzzles, paddles with balls attached and funny cardboard glasses with eyeballs painted on them. Aldo and Marty stood behind the prize table.

'Hurry up and take something,' Marty said in a gruff voice. He tried to stuff the glasses into A.J.'s hand. 'Move it along.'

Aldo nudged Marty. 'Give them a chance to decide what they want, Marty,' he suggested. 'How about a train whistle?' he asked, holding up a big wooden whistle in the shape of a train.

'Maybe,' said A.J.

'Paddleball is always good,' said Art. 'I'll take that.'

'Good choice,' Marty mumbled.

'I'll take the whistle,' A.J. decided. 'Thanks.'

'You're welcome.' It sounded strange to hear Mean Martin Bean say those words.

Kirk rushed to the prize booth with a handful of tickets.

'Well, if it isn't Kirk the Jer–' Marty stopped himself before he finished.

'Kirk the Basketball King!' said Aldo. 'Pick a prize.'

Kirk had enough tickets to get a flower with a bulb attached that could squirt water.

'Good choice,' said Marty. His voice sounded different. I suppose he wasn't used to saying nice things.

At last, Sayeh and Miranda, who had been watching Marty, finally came forward, clutching their prize tickets.

'Ladies, come and get your prizes,' said Aldo. 'Marty will help you. He likes to help. Right, Marty?'

'Here are some key chains,' Marty told the girls as they nervously stepped forward. 'Or maybe you'd like this noughts-and-crosses game.'

Miranda and Sayeh were obviously surprised that Marty was acting like a human being is supposed to act, but they handed over their tickets.

'Thanks, Marty,' said Miranda, taking the key chain.

Aldo grinned. So did Marty.

Everybody was having such a good time, I was tempted to open the lock-that-doesn't-lock and join the fun.

While I was thinking it over, Aldo blew a whistle and asked everybody to come to the 'centre ring' for the big show.

As I watched my classmates rush for their chairs, I realized that I had an excellent hamster's-eye view of the centre of the ring. There was no need to plan an escape after all.

Once everyone settled down, Aldo took centre stage and waved his top hat dramatically. 'Ladiezzzz and gentlemen, get ready to be dazzled by the one, the only, the Amazing Magic Mitch!'

Amazing Magic Mitch turned out to be a tall, skinny man also wearing a top hat. His long blond hair touched his shoulders. He had on an oversized black jacket with a red-and-white-striped T-shirt and wore huge red-rimmed glasses.

Aldo applauded and the rest of the audience joined in. Magic Mitch carried a table in one hand and a suitcase in the other. He put the suitcase on the table and pulled out a large black wand.

Now I understood. Amazing Magic Mitch was a magician! I'd heard about magic shows, but I'd never seen one before. My whiskers started to quiver as the act began.

He talked the whole time he performed his act. TALK-TALK-TALK! First, he started out with a card trick. He brought A.J. out of the audience and asked him to pick a card, memorize it and return it to the pack. The magician mixed up the cards and asked A.J. to pick another card. The card A.J. selected this time happened to be the EXACT card he had picked the first time!

'Think it's a trick pack?' asked the magician.

'Yes,' A.J. answered.

So Magic Mitch called Tabitha out of the audience. He asked her and A.J. to check the pack of cards to see that everything was normal. It was! Then Tabitha had to pick a card and memorize it. Mitch shuffled the cards all around again. When

Tabitha picked another card from the pack – you won't believe it – it was the exact same card she had picked before!

Everybody applauded, except me. This fellow seemed a little too crafty for me. I decided to keep a close eye on him.

Magic Mitch asked if he could borrow a coin from somebody. Marty volunteered one he had in his pocket. Imagine, a grown-up taking a coin from a kid!

Mitch rolled the coin up into a handkerchief and it disappeared completely, right before our eyes. He shook out the handkerchief, but the coin was gone! Marty gasped. Somebody should have warned Magic Mitch not to make Mean Bean angry.

The magician leaned over and asked, 'What's that in your ear?' He reached out to touch Marty's ear and produced a coin: the same one Marty had given him!

Now, I ask you, how can a coin disappear into thin air and then turn up in somebody's ear? This guy was CHEATING-CHEATING-CHEATING!

Next, Magic Mitch had the nerve to ask if the birthday boy had had any paper money for his birthday. Richie came up and gave the magician a brand-new banknote. You won't believe what Magic Mitch did with that note. He folded it all up, took out a pair of scissors and cut it into small pieces! That's the rudest thing I've ever seen. Even Og wouldn't do something like that. Richie's eyes were practically popping out of his head as Magic Mitch took the pieces of the note, put them in his fist and waved a magic wand. Nothing happened.

'I forgot to say the magic words!' he exclaimed. 'Eeny, meeny, miny, moe, you will see the money grow!' This time, when he opened his hand, the banknote was back, all in one piece again.

Thank goodness, or I think Richie would have been pretty angry!

Magic Mitch asked Sayeh and Mandy to help him with a trick where he cut up a rope, did some hocus-pocus and returned it in one piece.

And Art helped him make a glass of water disappear under a handkerchief. I mean a whole glass of water!

I would not invite this man to my house for supper, I can tell you.

Everybody seemed to like the show, though. They gasped and clapped at everything he did.

Finally, he announced the Big Moment! 'Ladies and gentlemen, at this point in the show, I usually make a rabbit appear out of my hat. But today, my rabbit is on strike. So I'm going to borrow your class hamster for this amazing trick.'

It took me a few seconds to realize that the class hamster was – gulp – me! Richie came over to my cage and gently picked me up, cupping me in his hands.

'Don't be scared, Humphrey. It's only a trick,' he whispered.

I knew that, but I didn't want to be cut up in pieces or disappear into thin air. No wonder the rabbit went on strike.

'Since Humphrey is already here, I can't pull him out of my hat. So instead, I will make him disappear into my hat!'

Magic Mitch first held his hat upside down and let anyone who wanted to come up and inspect it. Everybody agreed it appeared to be an ordinary hat.

Mitch took me from Richie and put me in the hat. It was DARK-DARK-DARK inside and I have to admit, I don't like dark places.

As he dropped me down, he pulled something with his finger and I fell into a secret compartment at the top of the hat. A false bottom came down over my head. I was trapped in a dark, scary place.

I could hear Magic Mitch's muffled voice saying, 'Abracadabra, Humphrey dear. I will make you disappear!'

Whoa! The magician turned the hat all the way over. Now I was lying on my back, feeling a little seasick.

'Humphrey! Where are you?' Magic Mitch called out.

He shook the hat to show that it was empty. Except it wasn't.

'Oooh,' I squeaked weakly as I bounced up and down, trapped in this stuffy cave.

I guess nobody heard me, not even Magic Mitch.

I could hear the sounds of kids gasping and shuffling around in their seats.

'Where's Humphrey?' I heard A.J. ask.

'Beats me,' said Magic Mitch. He turned the hat around and put it on his head. 'Want to see another trick?'

'Bring back Humphrey!' Richie said, in a voice as loud as A.J.'s.

'Humphrey who?' asked the magician. He started to do another trick. I couldn't see what he was doing, since I was completely in the dark.

Well, if Magic Mitch wasn't going to do anything about getting me out of that hat, I was going to do something for myself.

When I squinted my eyes, I could see a pinpoint of light above me. If I could see light, there must be an opening there. I crouched in the little space and reached up with my paws. I pushed. And I scratched. And I pushed some more. I may be small, but I'm strong for a hamster.

I could hear Magic Mitch repeating, 'Now you see it, now you don't. Which shell has the pea under it?'

'Bring back Humphrey!' more voices shouted, but Mitch ignored them.

Now I could see a lot more light. The top of the hat was opening from all my pushing. There was a space barely big enough for me to squeeze through. I pushed myself up with all my might and popped right out of the top of the hat! I could see my friends from Room 26, Richie's relatives, and also Marty Bean all staring up at me!

Magic Mitch kept going even though nobody paid any attention to him.

There was giggling, pointing, nudging and nodding. The giggling turned to chuckling, chortling, laughing and howling!

'Now you see it ... now you don't.' Mitch sounded confused. 'Everyone? Are you paying attention?'

I could hear my name being whispered around.

I stood up very tall as everyone stared at me. 'Greetings, one and all!' I squeaked as loudly as I could.

This produced shrieks of laughter. I took a bow.

The audience began to shout my name. They stamped their feet and clapped their hands as they chanted, 'Hum-phrey! Hum-phrey! Hum-phrey!'

'OK.' The magician sounded quite annoyed. 'I'll bring him back!'

He took his hat off and there I was, eyeball to

eyeball with Magic Mitch. He looked very pale. 'What are you doing? You've ruined my whole show!'

'It's my show now,' I squeaked to him.

'Next time, I'm bringing the rabbit,' he said glumly.

Nobody else heard him because all my friends continued to clap, stamp and cheer.

Aldo quickly entered the ring and said, 'Let's have a big round of applause for the Amazing Magic Mitch!'

Mitch waved his magic hat – which now had a hole in the top – and hurried away from Richie's basement as fast as he could.

The crowd kept applauding and cheering. I knew they were cheering for me.

> **A friend is a present you give yourself.**
> Robert Louis Stevenson, Scottish
> novelist and poet

13 Show Business, Snow Busines.

My classmates were still talking about the party on Monday. Even Mrs Brisbane chuckled when Richie told the whole story of my triumphant reappearance.

But there was something else to talk about: Og's surprise.

Bert Brisbane had built Og a genuine swimming pool! Instead of a large bowl of water, a whole section of the glass box was now water, while the rest of it was built up all around with lush green plants.

It was a terrific surprise and I felt just a tiny pang of green-eyed jealousy. Then I noticed that Og's grin looked more like a real smile this time. I guess we'd both had good weekends after all.

After everyone had admired the swimming pool, Mrs Brisbane got down to business. 'The Poetry

Festival is less than two weeks away. We've got to finalize our selections, memorize the poems, finish the artwork and make our Valentine's Day letterboxes.'

From that moment on, there was a mad flurry of activity. Some students retreated to the cloakroom to memorize their poems. Others drew pictures for the notice board while another group made Valentine letterboxes using glue, glitter, paint, crayons, buttons, lace and stickers.

Don't worry – Mrs Brisbane didn't forget to teach us maths, science, geography, social studies and spelling. (Believe me, she'd never do that.) But in between, my classmates worked like crazy on poetry and Valentines. Our classroom assistants, Mrs Hopper and Mrs Patel, came in to help for two days.

At night, it was just Og and me in Room 26. I wondered what he had done at the Brisbanes' house over the weekend as I watched him swimming and diving in his new pool. He could make a lot more noise splashing around in it. Each night, I got a little more annoyed, until one night I realized why. Here we were, side by side, but I still felt lonely. We had communicated a little and he'd helped me once, but I still wasn't sure if we were friends.

It was time to find out. I opened the

lock-that-doesn't-lock. Gathering up my courage, I walked over to his glass house and said, 'Hello, Og.'

Abruptly, Og turned towards me. I must admit, my hamster heart skipped a beat. Was he going to leap at me again?

'Look, maybe I haven't been much of a pal to you, Og. Maybe I was even a little jealous. But I'd like to try again.'

This time, instead of leaping, he dived into the water with a gigantic SPLASH! The water splashed up to the top of the box, through the screen, on to my nice dry fur! And if there's one thing hamsters hate, it's wet fur. My usually fluffy golden coat was drippy, droopy and dull. If Og was looking for attention, he was about to get it.

'Thanks for nothing, Og,' I squeaked. 'I just want you to know that I have a million friends, so I don't really care if you're my friend or not. So if you're thinking you should be my pal, just forget it!'

Og just stared at me with that same old smile.

'And remember that time you leaped at me?' I continued. 'You didn't even scare me.'

Not wanting to press my luck, I scampered back into my cage. I'd finally told him off, but I didn't feel better. Not one bit.

Thursday was the gloomiest day I'd ever seen outside. But inside Room 26, the students were far from gloomy. Heidi and Gail were best friends again. Tabitha was friendly with Seth, Sayeh, Miranda – everybody! The poems were coming along as well.

No one, except me, seemed to notice that it was GREY-GREY-GREY outside. In the afternoon, it began to snow. I hopped on to my wheel and watched giant circles of lace float to the ground.

That sounded so good, I wrote it in my notebook: 'Giant circles of lace.' Those words might turn into a poem some day.

The snow continued falling after school came out. It was pretty with all those lacy circles tumbling down from the sky. After a while, the lacy circles turned into a thick blanket of white.

It was so quiet, you could have heard a frog burp. Not that Og ever did. He was as silent as the snowflakes.

I knew something was terribly wrong when Aldo didn't turn up to clean that night. There were no cars in the car park and just one car parked on the street. It looked more like a giant snowball than a car.

I counted the hours until morning would arrive. The snow continued falling until it reached the top of the wheels on the parked car. The carpet of snow was beautiful, but the silence made my fur stand up on end. I missed A.J.'s loud voice, Mandy's complaints and Gail's giggles.

When the bell rang for the start of school on Friday, a funny thing happened: nobody turned up. Not Mrs Brisbane, not Garth, not Miranda, nobody. There were no cars in the car park, no buses pulling in.

The snow showed no sign of stopping. I was snowed in with Og the Frog!

> **A life without a friend is a life without sun.**
> French proverb

14 Oh No, More Snow!

It was eerie to hear the bell ring for morning break, lunch and afternoon break when there was no one at school except Og and me.

Staring out at all that snow gave me a chill. The temperature was dropping inside as well. What was it that Aldo had said about turning down the heat at night to save money? I felt even chillier as I realized there was no one around to turn the heat up again.

Luckily, I had my fur coat, my sleeping house and a nice pile of wood shavings I could crawl into to keep warm. I wondered how Og was doing with nothing more than four glass walls, some greenery and an unheated swimming pool.

I dozed for much of the day and nibbled on the stash of food I keep hidden in my sleeping nest. We hamsters are clever about saving up food in case of emergency. But my food dish was empty and my water was getting low.

Between naps, I gazed out of the window. There were still no cars on the street. In fact, I couldn't tell where the street ended and the pavement began. Everything was a solid sheet of white.

Og was quiet most of the time and the crickets were silent too. I was BORED-BORED-BORED all alone in the classroom. I even missed maths class! Finally, I hopped on to my wheel for some lively exercise. That warmed me up, but it also made me hungry. When I checked my stash of food, the only thing left was a limp tomato stalk!

The bell signalling the end of school finally rang. I wondered what my classmates were doing. A.J. was probably watching TV with his family. Garth and Andy would be playing video games. I figured Miranda was cuddling up with Clem. (Didn't his bad breath bother her?) Sayeh was no doubt helping her mum care for her younger brother. And Mrs Brisbane was probably bustling around her warm, toasty kitchen while Mr Brisbane built a birdbox.

They were all warm, all cosy and all well-fed! They were definitely not worrying about me. Or Og.

I wasn't helping myself by thinking of these things. I decided to work on my poem. What rhymes with 'gloom'? Doom!

I slipped my notebook and pencil out of their hiding place behind my mirror and burrowed down into my pile of wood shavings to keep warm.

I promptly fell asleep. It was night-time when I woke up.

'Hey, Og, do you think Aldo will come tonight?' I asked my neighbour.

Og didn't answer. Aldo didn't come. The snow kept falling.

Around midnight, I heard a funny whirring sound and looked out of the window. A huge machine, much bigger than a car, crept down the street like a giant yellow snail with an orange light spinning around on top. It rolled along slowly, then disappeared.

Three hours later, it returned from the opposite direction and disappeared again.

'Did you see that, Og?' I squeaked loudly.

He was definitely ignoring me, and I didn't blame him. I'd said terrible things to him, things he probably understood. Guilt made me feel even colder.

'Og, I didn't mean it when I said I didn't care if you were my friend,' I called out from my cage. 'I'll forgive you for splashing me if you'll forgive me for saying those things. OK?'

'Boing?' I think he meant 'OK,' but there was something odd about the way Og sounded. Maybe he was hungry, like me. Then I recalled that he didn't need to eat as often as I do. Frogs have all the luck.

·ö·

The next morning, the snow stopped falling. But the ground was covered and there were still no cars or people to be seen, except for that parked snowball – I mean car.

Even if it hadn't snowed, nobody would have come to school, because it was Saturday. One week ago today, I was starring in Magic Mitch's show. Now I was alone (almost), COLD-COLD-COLD, hungry and forgotten.

All my life, some human had brought me food and water and cleaned my cage. I'd been well cared for. I'd never had to fend for myself. But I was a clever and capable hamster. It was time for me to take care of myself like my wild hamster ancestors, the ones who lived in the forests with piles of leaves and pine cones. And all the fruits and nuts they could collect.

Hunger must have clouded my brain because it hadn't occurred to me until that moment that all my hamster food was right there on the table. Yummy things like hay, mealworms, grains and vitamin drops. All I had to do was help myself!

I opened the lock-that-doesn't-lock and stumbled out of my cage.

'Og, are you OK?' I called out.

'Boing,' he replied weakly. It had been a while since he'd eaten too. And I remembered Mrs Brisbane talking about how important it was for frogs to have fresh water.

'I'm going to get some food,' I explained. 'Maybe I can find some mealworms for you. I don't think I can get into the cricket cabinet.' Lucky for the crickets.

'Boing.' Og sounded even weaker this time. And he didn't look as green as usual. For a frog, that's not good.

I rushed across the top of the table, slightly faint from hunger. And there they were: a great big bag of Nutri-Nibbles, a taller bag of Hamster Hay and a giant jar of Mighty Mealworms. Yum! Of course, getting from the table to the top of those containers was a big problem for a small hamster. If I climbed up the bag of Nutri-Nibbles, for example, I would be in serious danger of falling into the bag and getting trapped there. Even though I love Nutri-Nibbles, I didn't want to spend my last minutes on earth being crushed by them.

No, the only sensible approach was brute force. I decided to take a run at the bag and knock it over. The treats would tumble out and I could eat to my heart's content.

I took a deep breath and ran at the bag, yelling 'Charge!'

It didn't quite work out according to my plan. I hit the bag with all my might and it tipped a little. Unfortunately, then the bag tipped back the other way and crashed down on top of me!

I wasn't crushed, but I was trapped underneath the bag of treats. There was a little air space around me and I could see a glimmer of light. I could breathe too. I just couldn't get out.

What I could do was yell. 'Help! I'm trapped!' I squeaked, although the bag muffled the sound.

I'm not sure why I was yelling. 'Help me, please!' probably sounded like 'SQUEAK-SQUEAK-SQUEAK!'

I squeaked anyway, and waited.

What was that I heard? 'Boing, boing, boing! BOING, BOING, BOING!! *BOING, BOING, BOING*!!!' Followed by a large crash!

I couldn't imagine how Og thought that all that noise would help me. Then I heard a new sound: bop-bop-bop. Soon, Og was grinning at me through the slit of light.

That crazy old lump of a frog had managed to hop all the way out of his house, and he'd come to save me! He started leaping at the bag, each time hitting it harder and harder. The bag shifted and the space around me started to open up as I crawled towards him.

Og kept bashing the bag, screaming, 'Screee!

Screee!' This was a whole new Og and a whole new sound.

The space got bigger and bigger and I crawled along until I could reach out and grab Og. Although I was weak from hunger and all that effort, I managed to grab on to Og's back just as the bag shifted again, flattening out. I was GLAD-GLAD-GLAD I wasn't underneath it any more.

'Screee!' Og repeated. I pulled myself up on to Og's back and he hopped away from the bag.

What a thrill! I was rocking and rolling on his back, like a cowboy riding a bucking bronco! 'Yee-haw!' I yelled. 'Go, Og! Go, Frog!'

'Screee!' he yelled.

All of a sudden, the lights came on and I heard footsteps.

'Oh no! Look at that, they're out of their cages.' It was Mrs Brisbane. 'They knocked the food over. They must be starving, poor things!'

'Smart little critters,' said Mr Morales, chuckling. '*Muy inteligente.*'

I hardly recognized those two, bundled up in heavy coats and woolly hats with huge scarves almost covering their faces.

'How on earth did they get out?' Mrs Brisbane wondered.

'Maybe somebody didn't lock Humphrey's cage tightly,' said the headmaster. 'And I suppose the frog hopped out of his tank. Look, he pushed the lid off.'

So I have a lock-that-doesn't-lock and Og has a top-that-he-can-pop!

'Never fear, Aldo's here!' another voice yelled out.

A bundled-up Aldo hurried into the room. 'Are they OK? The snowplough didn't clean our street until half an hour ago. I was going to walk over here, but the radio said it was too dangerous to go out.'

'I know,' said Mrs Brisbane. 'Bert and I have been worried sick. If I'd known the storm was coming, I would have taken them home with me. And everybody's rung me. All the parents, Angie Loomis – everybody.'

Mrs Brisbane put me back into my cage and gave me a handful of Nutri-Nibbles. Mr Morales put Og back into his box and fed him some icky crickets (gag!). Aldo went to get us both fresh water.

'It's too cold in here for Og,' Mr Morales said. 'He pulled through all right, but I'm going to buy him a heater.'

More footsteps clomped across the floor. 'We came as soon as we got shovelled out!' said Miranda as she, Amy and Abby arrived.

'The girls have been worried all day,' said Amy.

We hadn't been forgotten after all. Heidi's mum,

Garth's dad and Sayeh and her dad turned up too, every one of them worried about Og and me.

I wanted to thank them, but it's not polite to talk with your mouth full.

They all asked to take us home for the rest of the weekend, but Mrs Brisbane was quite firm. 'I'm going to be selfish this time. I'm taking them home with me. My husband would never forgive me if I didn't.'

Mr Morales told everyone to be VERY-VERY-VERY careful on the drive back home. He and Aldo helped Mrs Brisbane prepare our houses for the trip.

Finally, my tummy felt full. 'Og?' I squeaked. 'Thank you, my friend! Does this mean you forgive me?'

'Boing!' he answered. Which was an extremely nice thing for a frog to say.

> **Real friendship is shown in times of trouble; prosperity is full of friends.**
> Ralph Waldo Emerson, American poet and essayist

15 Poetry Festivity

Bert Brisbane was waiting at the door for us. 'Hurry on in. It's freezing!' he said.

Mr Morales helped Mrs Brisbane carry in our houses and all the bags of food and bedding. 'Who knows how long they'll have to stay?' he said.

Mrs Brisbane went to make a pot of tea, and soon Mr Brisbane was cleaning Og's tank. Mr Morales may be the Most Important Person at Longfellow School, but the headmaster rolled up his sleeves and cleaned out my cage. He didn't even complain about what was in my potty corner. (He did wear gloves and washed his hands afterwards.)

'This is a good lesson for all of us,' said Mrs Brisbane as she brought in a tray of steaming cups of tea, a plate of biscuits and some yummy pieces of broccoli and lettuce for me. 'If you decide to have a pet, you have to take total responsibility.'

Mr Morales munched on a biscuit. 'I think they took responsibility for themselves. How on earth did such small creatures knock down that big bag?'

'I was wondering about that too,' said Mrs Brisbane. 'I think it was teamwork.'

'A frog and a hamster? Never heard of such a thing,' said Bert. 'I really wish I'd seen those two.' He smiled and shook his head. 'I always knew that Humphrey was sharp as a needle, but now we know there's a lot going on in Og's head too.'

'Boing!' Og croaked, and he lunged at the side of his glass box.

Mrs Brisbane chuckled. 'He's feeling better. Looks like he wants to play a game of leapfrog.'

Leapfrog is a *game*? Had I been wrong about Og since that very first night? Instead of trying to scare me, he wanted to play?

Like Mr Brisbane, I wasn't sure what went on in Og's head, but he had some good ideas, like rescuing me. He even had another sound he could make. Nobody knew it but me, and that made me feel kind of special. Like a friend.

The sun came out that afternoon and so did the snowploughs. While the gardens were still covered with snow, the streets were clear and cars travelled freely again.

Across the street from the Brisbanes, two children built a snowman. Inside the Brisbane house, I was more than happy to run mazes and play hide-and-squeak with Bert for old time's sake. Og watched from his glass house, but said very little.

·ö·

By Monday, the roads had improved enough for everyone to go back to school. Thank goodness, because the Poetry Festival was coming up on Friday and there was still a lot of work to do.

Some of the students had worked on memorizing their poems or writing them out at home over the long weekend. Most had not.

Garth Tugwell had changed poems three times. On Monday, he changed again. Mrs Brisbane sent him to the cloakroom to memorize his new selection.

Mrs Brisbane surprised Kirk by asking for his help. 'You've been a lot better lately about knowing when to be funny and when to be quiet,' she said. 'Now I need your help. We don't want this Poetry Festival to be too serious. We want it to be fun. Would you introduce the poems for us?'

Kirk's whole face lit up. 'Sure!'

'Be sure to make it funny,' she told him.

By the end of the day on Tuesday, the notice board was covered with illustrated poems the students had copied out. Along the edge of the board were cut-out pictures of famous poets, from Longfellow to a man named Shakespeare and a lady named Emily Dickinson.

Late in the day on Wednesday, my classmates finished their Valentine letterboxes. What they did with ordinary cardboard boxes was excellent! Some of them were covered with red hearts, glitter and pieces of lace. Others were covered with buttons and lots of paint. Garth's had a big dinosaur on the side. Miranda's letterbox had cut-out pictures of her family pasted on: her mum, dad, Abby, Amy, baby Ben and (yes) Clem. Tabitha's letterbox had pictures of basketballs, footballs and soccer balls glued across the outside.

Then – SURPRISE – Mandy presented Og with a green box with pictures of frogs and insects all over it. And A.J. gave me a box covered in golden, furry-looking material. (It wasn't real fur. I checked.)

As nice as that was, I felt SAD-SAD-SAD because no matter how many Valentines I received, there was no way I could make Valentines for everyone in the class. How could I let them know how much I valued their friendship?

I was still feeling low when Aldo arrived on Wednesday night. He was in an unusually good mood.

'It's a beautiful evening, gentlemen. And I have good news to share with you!' he announced as he wheeled in his trolley.

'I could use some good news, Aldo!' I squeaked back.

'Boing!' added Og.

Aldo pulled up a chair next to my cage. Instead of taking out his sandwich (or a treat for me), he pulled out a piece of paper.

'Behold my first mark from college. A test in psychology.' (I wondered if he was in the same class as Natalie the babysitter.)

'My mark, as you can plainly see . . .' Aldo held the paper up to my cage. 'Is an A! Can you believe it, my friends?'

'Three cheers for Aldo!' I squeaked as I hopped on to my wheel for a joyful spin.

'I haven't shown this to Maria yet. I'm saving it for her Valentine's present. Along with some flowers and sweets, of course. I think this mark will be her favourite gift.' Aldo leaned back and smiled with satisfaction.

Og dived into his pool with a huge splash. I think a little water got on Aldo, but he didn't seem to mind.

'Splash away, Og my friend,' Aldo said. 'It makes a happy sound.'

Og splashed because he was happy? All I'd

thought about the splashing was that it was irritating!

Aldo was grinning from ear to ear, almost like a frog. 'You see before you a happy man. There's nothing better in the world than to have someone to share good news – and even bad news – with. You see, Maria is my wife, but she's also my best friend.'

I stopped spinning because I felt a little dizzy. I'd learned a bit about friendship this year by watching my classmates in Room 26. There were friends who got really angry but made up afterwards. There were friends who stuck together through thick and thin. There were friends who reached out to you even when you didn't think you needed a friend.

There were friends who would actually rescue you when you were in trouble. There were new friends, old friends, silver and gold friends.

Later that night, I was SORRY-SORRY-SORRY I'd ever doubted Og was my friend. I hadn't understood that sometimes a frog feels jealous and sometimes he feels splash-happy. But he had come through for me when I needed help. So how do you say thank you to a frog?

I decided to write a poem. Not just a 'roses are red, frogs are green' poem, but a poem that said what I really felt.

I pulled out my notebook and started to write.

The next day was spent rehearsing for the Poetry Festival and straightening up the room. (Boy, those kids' tables can get pretty messy.) I didn't pay much attention. I was hunkered down in my sleeping house, writing my hamster heart out.

Friday was Valentine's Day and everyone was excited. In the morning, the students 'posted' their Valentine cards in a big box on Mrs Brisbane's desk. During break, the teacher sorted out the cards and delivered them, humming happily as she dropped them into the boxes.

After break, the students opened their cards. There was a lot of giggling and even some crunching, since Mrs Brisbane had also dropped sugar hearts into all the letterboxes.

Out of the blue, A.J. shouted, 'Hey, hold on!' That got everyone's attention. 'I got a card from Martin Bean!'

Seth groaned loudly.

'No, listen. He says he's sorry,' A.J. explained.

'I got one too!' said Garth.

Miranda and Heidi had also got 'I'm sorry' cards from Marty.

'But he's so mean,' Mandy blurted.

'People can change,' said Mrs Brisbane. 'I think it must have been quite difficult for Martin to write those cards, and he gave them to me to deliver. Maybe it's time to give him a second chance.'

Whew, giving Mean Bean a second chance wouldn't be easy. Yet I recalled that once he got started, he was actually pretty nice when he handed out prizes at the birthday party. Maybe Aldo's talk with him had done some good. No wonder he got that A in psychology.

'I'll give him a second chance!' I exclaimed. Of course, it came out 'Squeak-squeak-squeak.'

'I haven't forgotten you, Humphrey,' said Mrs Brisbane. She came over to help Og and me with our letterboxes. We received cards from all the students in class. Each one was special, but the one I remember the most was from Miranda.

Though 'hamster' doesn't have a rhyme.
I love you. Humphrey. all the time.

She'd worked out how to write a poem with the word 'hamster' in it after all!

I had one more card in my letterbox than Og. It was from Brazil! Yes, Ms Mac had remembered me with a teeny little card that said, 'Humphrey, you will always be a special friend. Love, Ms Mac.'

She'd sent a letter to the whole class as well, with greetings from her pupils in Brazil.

Wonderful as it was to receive those cards, I kept

one eye on the clock all morning, because I had a special mission to accomplish during lunch.

A hamster's work is never done.

The bell finally rang and the students left, which was good. But Mrs Brisbane stayed behind, which was bad. She busily rearranged all the chairs into a big half-circle. She picked scraps of paper off the floor and straightened a few tables. Wasn't this woman going to eat?

At last, she glanced up at the clock, picked up her lunch bag and hurried out of the room. I didn't have much time, so I tore a page out of my notebook, jiggled the lock-that-doesn't-lock, flung open the door and slid down the leg of the table.

Og started boinging in alarm, but I didn't have time to explain.

I raced across the floor as fast as my legs would carry me, straight to Mrs Brisbane's desk. When I got there, I gasped with surprise. My plan was to climb up her chair and take a giant leap on to the desk. It was dangerous and risky, but sometimes you have to be bold! However, the teacher had ruined everything by moving her chair FAR-FAR-FAR away from her desk, into the circle of other chairs.

Even worse, her desk didn't have legs to climb up. It was a solid block of wood.

My Big Plan was completely spoiled!

The clock ticked away. My only option was to put

the piece of paper on the floor near her desk and scramble back on to the table. I grabbed the cord from the blinds and began to swing back and forth until I got up to the top of the table. I took the final leap and scurried back to my cage, pulling the door shut behind me.

'Boing-boing-boing!' croaked Og.

'You'll understand soon,' I told him. 'I hope.'

After lunch, Mrs Brisbane returned to the classroom, followed by her other students. The classroom assistants arrived with juice and biscuits. Next, the other parents entered. Everyone was so busy saying hello and admiring the decorations that I lost track of Mrs Brisbane.

I could hear her, though. 'Ladies and gentlemen, if you could take your seats, we're ready for the Poetry Festival to begin.' She talked about what we'd been studying and all the hard work we'd put in. Then she turned the celebration over to Kirk Chen.

Kirk was in good form. He introduced each student with a short poem. The rhymes were funny, but they didn't hurt anybody's feelings. For instance, when it was Heidi's turn, Kirk said, 'Here's something fun by Heidi Hopper. When it comes to poems, you can't top her!'

He introduced Tabitha by saying, 'Tabitha's new, but boy, can she rhyme. We hope she stays a long, long time.'

And for A.J.'s poem he said, 'A.J.'s poem makes him proud, so don't be surprised if he speaks real loud.'

(A.J. did, too.)

I was PROUD-PROUD-PROUD of my classmates as one by one they stood in front of the room and recited their poems. Heidi recited the frog poem she wrote. Instead of her Smiley poem, Tabitha performed a funny poem about a baseball player named Casey. Sayeh recited the dove poem. Pay-Attention-Art lost his place in his poem, but he started over again and did fine. If anybody forgot a word, Mrs Brisbane whispered it and nobody seemed to notice.

The parents clapped heartily for each and every poem. I did too!

Then my heart sank as Mrs Brisbane said, 'That concludes this year's Poetry Festival. I hope you'll all stay for refreshments.'

My Plan had failed utterly! I glanced over at Og. He was still smiling, but he didn't know what I had planned.

But Mrs Brisbane kept talking. 'I have one more

poem I'd like to share. I found this scrap of paper on the floor as you arrived. I think it expresses the feelings the children in this room have for each other. It's very tiny and a little hard to read, but I'll try.'

A friend doesn't have to be a work of art.
Just have a heart.

A friend doesn't need to have fur or hair
To care.

A friend doesn't have a thing to do
But like you.

A friend doesn't need to say a word
To be heard.

It's not so hard to be a friend
In the end.

The room was silent until Heidi's mum started the applause and everyone joined in.

'There's a scratchy kind of scribbling at the bottom. I can't make out the name,' said Mrs Brisbane. 'Would the pupil who wrote this like to stand up and identify himself or herself?'

I was standing up all right. And I squeaked at the

top of my voice, 'I wrote it! I wrote it for Og! It's my Valentine to him!'

'Sounds like Humphrey knows who wrote it,' Mr Golden joked, and everybody laughed. Everybody except Og.

'Boing-boing!' he shouted, hopping up and down. At last, I'd got through to him. And now I knew exactly what he was saying.

'You're welcome, Og,' I replied. 'You're welcome, you grinning, green, lumpy, bumpy, hairless, goggle-eyed, cricket-eating friend. You're entirely welcome.'

Later that night, I looked over at Og as he dived into his swimming pool with a giant splash! He looked the same as ever, yet everything was different. What had seemed like a sneery leer was really a friendly grin. The splashing that once annoyed me made me feel good, because I knew Og was HAPPY-HAPPY-HAPPY. And a lunge that once scared me just meant Og wanted to play a game.

Sometimes humans are hard to understand, especially when they act mean, like Marty Bean, or get crabby, like Abby. But with patience (and a little psychology), you can usually figure them out.

It's the same with frogs. And even hamsters.

I'd made a few mistakes, but I'd managed to keep my old friends in Room 26 and make a new one too.

Suddenly, my heart went 'BOING!' as I thought about my shiny-silver new friend.

My friend Og.

Of what shall a man be proud,
if he is not proud of his friends?
Robert Louis Stevenson,
Scottish novelist and poet

Humphrey's Guide to the Care and Feeding of Friends

1 If you act like a jerk and tease people, you won't have any friends. Guaranteed.

2 If you do the opposite, and are nice to people, you'll have friends. It might take a while, but you'll have friends.

3 If you act like a jerk to your friends and they get angry, but you're REALLY-REALLY-REALLY sorry and let your friends know it, they will probably forgive you.

4 People don't always think so, but boys and girls can be friends.

5 Sometimes you may want to be friends with somebody, but that person (or frog) doesn't want to be friends back. That seems SAD-SAD-SAD, but it's not, because

there are other people out there waiting to be friends with you. You just have to look for them. Keep looking – don't give up!

6 A friend is someone you like to be with and you don't even have to talk. Or squeak.

7 Friendship has its own language. Even if you don't understand the words your friend says, you can understand the meaning.

8 You might not know somebody's your friend until he has a problem and you realize you care.

p.s. Tegucigalpa is the capital of Honduras, a country in Central America. Look it up on the map!

Don't forget – you can keep up to date
with all of Humphrey's news, share your
jokes and pet pictures, and download
activity sheets at:

www.funwithhumphrey.com

What will Humphrey get up to next?

Find out in
Trouble According to Humphrey . . .

1 Before the Trouble

'Welcome to our brand-new town!'

Mrs Brisbane's voice woke me from my cosy afternoon doze. Was I dreaming when I heard her mention a new town? Had we moved while I was having my afternoon nap?

Staying awake is a constant problem for a classroom hamster like me. After all, hamsters are nocturnal, which means we're sleepier in the daytime than at night. I always try hard to keep up with my fellow students in Room 26. However, I'd spent the long holiday weekend at Kirk Chen's house. His whole family is funny like he is. It was hard to get much sleeping done there since I was laughing all the time.

But with Mrs Brisbane's announcement, I was suddenly wide awake. I looked around and saw that I was in the same old Room 26 in my same old cage on the table next to the window. Og the Frog's same old glass house sat next to mine.

Around me were the usual tables and the familiar students like Speak-up-Sayeh, Lower-Your-Voice-A.J. and Wait-For-The-Bell-Garth. The same teacher, Mrs Brisbane, stood in front of the class.

I guess I wasn't the only one who was confused. 'What new town?' Heidi Hopper asked.

'Please Raise-Your-Hand-Heidi,' Mrs Brisbane said. 'Since we are studying how communities work, I thought it was time to create our own community of Room Twenty-Sixville.'

Whew! I was relieved because I love our classroom right where it is and I wasn't in the mood to move.

'BOING!' said Og in his twangy voice. I guess he was relieved, too.

'We've been studying what makes a community – right?' asked Mrs Brisbane.

YES-YES-YES, I'd learned a lot about communities recently. First, I learned that there are two Ms in the word. I'm trying to remember that in case it shows up in a spelling test in the future. I'd learned that a community isn't just a place on a map, it's also made up of the people who live there. (I'm sure Mrs Brisbane meant to include animals, too, but forgot to mention us.)

I'd also learned that everyone's job helps the community in some way or another. There are police officers and firefighters to protect us and people who sell books or clothes or even sell wonderful pets like me! After all, I came from Pet-O-Rama, a shop in our community. There are people who grow and sell food and people who keep the streets clean and people who keep the classrooms clean, like Aldo, our caretaker. There are also doctors who people go to when they are ill and dentists who help people keep their teeth healthy.

Then there's the biggest job of all: teacher. Teachers like Mrs Brisbane help us learn about things we wouldn't know otherwise, such as the life cycle of a frog (though I still can't picture Og as a tadpole), writing poems and adding and subtracting big numbers. Sometimes my paw gets tired from writing down really long problems in the tiny notebook I keep hidden behind my mirror, but I keep writing anyway because it's important.

My mind wandered while Mrs Brisbane continued to talk about all we'd learned until I realized – oh no! – I wasn't listening at all! If I kept day-dreaming, I'd end up like Pay-Attention-Art-Patel, who only paid attention in class about half the time and whose recent marks, I'm sorry to say, were dreadful. Not at all like Speak-Up-Sayeh, the quiet girl who always pays attention and gets the best marks in the class (better than mine, I have to admit).

There I was again, my mind wandering to Art's problems instead of listening to Mrs Brisbane. I hopped up on my ladder and vowed to listen to every word she said.

'It's one thing to talk about a community and another thing to be part of one,' the teacher was saying. 'So that's why I decided to create our own community here. We'll lay out our town right in this classroom and everyone will have a job.'

Garth's hand shot up. 'Will we get paid?'

'Not in money. You will get points for doing your jobs correctly and extra points for doing your job especially well.'

Another hand went up. Mrs Brisbane called on Don't-Complain-Mandy-Payne. 'I don't like the name Room Twenty-Sixville,' she said.

I don't think Mandy realizes how much she complains.

Mrs Brisbane smiled. 'Do you have a better name?'

Mandy scratched the tip of her nose. 'Brisbaneville?'

'I don't want to name it after me,' said the teacher. 'Besides, there already is a famous town named Brisbane. It's in Australia and they pronounce it "Brisbin".'

'Maybe we should call it Boringville,' a low voice muttered.

'I-Heard-That-Kirk,' Mrs Brisbane said. 'It was a rude thing to say. Do you really think school is boring?'

'Sorry. I was making a joke.' I believed him because Kirk is such a big joker. He's also a quick thinker. 'Og looks pretty bored,' he said.

All heads – including mine – turned to gaze at Og, who sat completely motionless on his rock, staring into space without even blinking.

'Og is a frog,' Mrs Brisbane said. 'He always looks that way.'

I'm never completely sure what Og thinks, but *I* don't think Room 26 is a boring place at all. I decided to squeak up on the subject, so I leaped up and grabbed onto a leafy tree branch our teacher's husband, Mr Brisbane, had put in my cage. He was always adding new and interesting things to my home, like my ladders and a large cage extension.

Mrs Brisbane turned towards me. 'Humphrey certainly doesn't seem bored.'

I loudly squeaked 'NO-NO-NO,' and jumped to another branch.

'Let's call it Humphreyville!' That was definitely A.J.'s loud voice and this time he forgot to raise his hand, too.

'Humphreyville!' Voices burst out from around the room, along with chuckles and giggles.

'Humphreyville?' Mrs Brisbane thought it over.

Unfortunately, it was hard to think because Gail had gone into one of her giggling fits.

'Stop-Giggling-Gail,' said the teacher. 'Please. Now what do the rest of you think? Miranda?'

Miranda Golden – or Golden-Miranda as I like to think of her – didn't hesitate a bit. 'I love the name!'

'Sayeh, what do you think?' For once, quiet Speak-Up-Sayeh didn't have any trouble speaking up. 'Yes, it sounds like a real place.'

'What is it again?' Pay-Attention-Art asked.

'Humphreyville,' Sayeh told him.

'I never heard of a town named after a hamster,' said Art.

Well, I may be a hamster but I'm no ordinary hamster. I am an exceptionally cute golden hamster (I've been told) who happens to know how to read and write. Not that anyone knows about that except me. Or the fact that my cage has a lock-that-doesn't-lock so I can come and go as I please when no one's looking.

'Humphreyville,' Art repeated. 'Sounds pretty good.'

I saw lots of heads nodding and heard murmuring around the class that sounded as if people were agreeing.

Imagine – a whole town named after me! I leaped onto my wheel and began spinning with joy.

'Why don't we take a vote?' asked Mrs Brisbane. 'All those in favour of naming our community "Humphreyville", raise your hands.'

While I was spinning, I could see hands going up. Even Heidi remembered to raise her hand. Every hand was raised except one: Tabitha's. I stopped spinning.

Tabitha was the new girl in our class and I thought she liked me. I'd even helped her make friends with Seth, although she didn't actually know it. I have some sneaky, squeaky ways of making things like that happen.

'Tabitha, do you have another suggestion for a name?' Mrs Brisbane asked.

'No,' said Tabitha. 'I like Humphreyville. I'm just afraid Og will be jealous.'

Jealous! I hadn't thought about that, even though when Mrs Brisbane brought Og in as a second classroom pet, I'd been jealous of him. It's embarrassing to admit it, but it's true.

'That's something to think about, isn't it? After all, if we named our community "Tabithaville", the other students might be jealous,' the teacher agreed.

'Yeah, and it's hard to say,' Heidi blurted out.

'Heidi, you simply must remember to raise your hand!' Mrs Brisbane had helped a lot of students to change their bad habits. Somehow, she'd never been able to get Heidi to remember to raise her hand.

'Now, class, why don't we let Og decide?' The teacher walked over to the frog's glass house. 'Og, do you vote for Humphreyville?'

I wasn't expecting much, because I'd learned that Og, being a frog, has an unusual way of expressing himself. His 'BOINGS' are nothing like the energetic squeaks of a hamster or the giggles and shouts of the kids. In fact, sometimes Og doesn't communicate at all. Still, he and I had learned to be friends. So I wouldn't have been surprised if he just continued to sit motionless, as usual.

But that's not what he did at all! Instead, he started leaping up and down on his rock, splashing water up onto Mrs Brisbane's chin. 'BOING-BOING-BOING!' he twanged as only Og can do.

The students laughed uproariously. Even Mrs Brisbane chuckled as she wiped the water off. 'Thank you for your vote, Og. Now let's try again. All in favour of naming our new community "Humphreyville", raise your hands.'

This time every hand went up, including Tabitha's. Whew! She liked me after all. Og stopped leaping and splashing and sat quietly on his rock again.

Mrs Brisbane looked pleased. 'Welcome, class, to the town of Humphreyville!' She wrote the name on the board in great big letters. 'And to keep track of the progress of our town, we'll be starting a daily newspaper. I think *The Humphreyville Herald* would be a good name, don't you?'

My friends all agreed!

My heart hopped around in my chest like a happy frog. Had any hamster ever been honoured like this before? Probably not. I decided right then and there that I would try to remain as humble as possible and do whatever I could to make Humphreyville the BEST-BEST-BEST town in the world!

I jumped on my wheel and spun for a while until I realized that Mrs Brisbane was still talking. 'There's a whole lot more to building a community than finding a name.'

I stopped spinning and started listening.

'What's the first thing you need when you move to a new place?'

I knew what I'd need: a cage. There was no point in my raising my paw since I never get called on, but a lot of other hands went up. Mrs Brisbane called on Repeat-It-Please-Richie. 'A car,' he said. 'Or a truck to carry all the stuff you're moving.'

'What if you didn't own anything at all?' asked the teacher. 'What would you need first?'

'Bargainmart!' Richie said. Everybody laughed. I figured Bargainmart must be some kind of shop, like Pet-O-Rama.

'I think you're jumping ahead. Tabitha, did you have your hand up?'

Tabitha nodded. 'You'd need a place to live. A house.'

'Or a tent!' Heidi blurted out.

'Very good,' said Mrs Brisbane, ignoring Heidi's outburst. 'Something like a house. Your first assignment is to design a place that represents where you would live in the town. You can draw a picture or make a model out of clay or build it out of cardboard. Be creative and think about what kind of home you'd like for yourself in Humphreyville.'

The bell rang. 'We'll have maths after break and then we'll get to work on your homes.'

Break is a time when my classmates all go out and play. It must be fun because my friends usually come back laughing and joking. At this time of year – late February – they also come back with rosy cheeks and red noses.

I always stay inside and try to get some exercise, climbing my ladder or spinning on my wheel. I must admit, sometimes I go into my sleeping hut for a nice nap because remember, I am nocturnal.

On this day, when Mrs Brisbane wasn't paying attention, I sneaked my notebook into my sleeping hut and thought about what kind of house I'd build. I loved my cage, but sometimes I'd think about the fancy houses they sold at Pet-O-Rama. One was a

Chinese pagoda and one was like a TALL-TALL-TALL castle. Ms Mac, the supply teacher and superb human being who first brought me from the pet shop to Room 26 of Longfellow School, couldn't afford one of those, which was okay with me. Anything Ms Mac did was fine with me. Yet, it was fun to think about my perfect house.

After all, if you have a whole town named after you, you should have a nice place to live!

NEW TOWN IN ROOM 26 TO BE NAMED AFTER CLASSROOM HAMSTER
Houses will be going up in Humphreyville within a week. teacher predicts.
The Humphreyville Herald

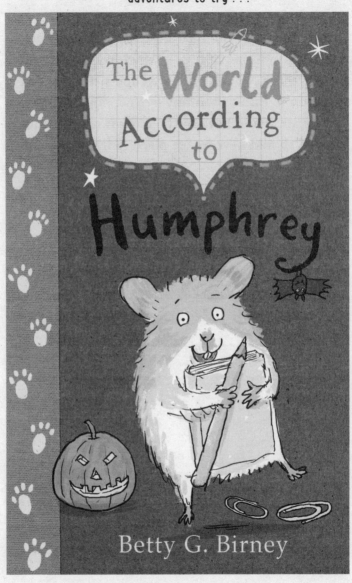

The World According to Humphrey

Betty G. Birney

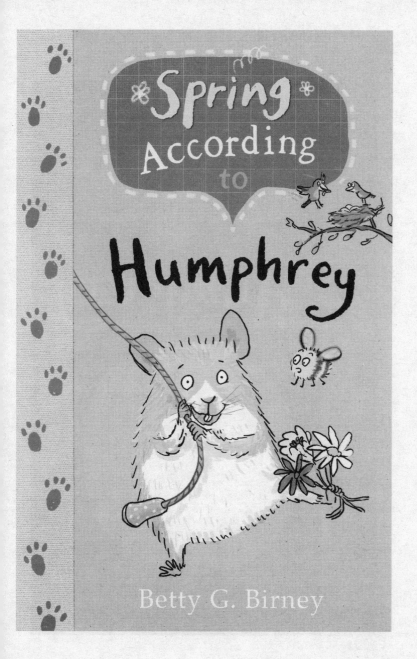

Spring According to Humphrey

Betty G. Birney

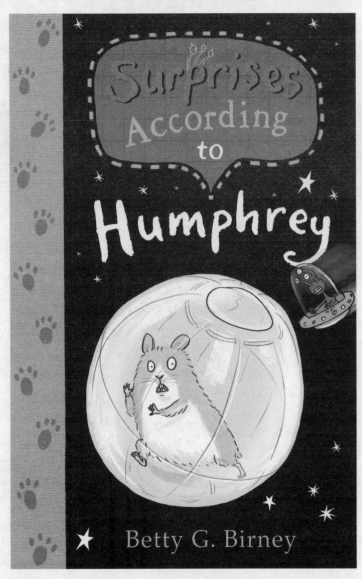